PROLOGUE

STONE

SEVEN MONTHS AGO

THE EXCITEMENT OF CALE AND Riley announcing that they're having a baby kept us all out late, celebrating. As soon as I got off the stage for the night, we took off to *Fortunes* and closed the bar down with the rest of the gang.

It was a crazy night and the way that Sage had been looking at me and fucking me with her eyes, she's been making it impossible to keep my dick in control.

Sage and I made a decision last month to cool off on our messing around, before things could get too complicated, but her flirting and teasing is making it impossible to keep my hands to myself when all I want is to have them all over her beautiful body, touching her in ways that'll make her scream.

The deal when she moved in a year ago was that we'd be roommates and occasional fuckbuddies to help satisfy each other's needs.

No sleeping in the same bed.

No fucking without a condom.

No fucking twice in the same month.

No becoming attached.

No jealousy.

No commitment.

Just for fun.

With a woman as beautiful as Sage, following the rules isn't that damn simple. Trust me, it takes every restraint a man has. Especially when his dick is practically standing tall twenty-four-seven.

Fuck me . . . I want her all of the time.

We've been at it for too long for her to believe that we can keep it up and just stay friends. I understand why she's afraid of commitment and I don't blame her. She's had it rough, so I'll do my best to respect that.

We're both young and have a lot of shit going on. Not to mention; I'm a male fucking stripper. I'm sure that doesn't keep her warm at night.

Maybe backing off is best for both of us.

We've just made it back to the house and Sage hasn't taken her hands off me since we left the bar. It's been weeks since the last time we've had sex and I can't deny that my cock wants nothing more than to sink into her tight little pussy, making her scream my name as I claim her body.

There's nothing I love more than my name on her lips, moaning.

Laughing, Sage straddles my lap and wraps her arms around my neck. "I've been thinking about touching you all night since seeing you on that stage. Do you realize how damn sexy you are and how hard you're making this strictly roommates thing?"

Smiling, I lean in and suck her bottom lip into my mouth, softly biting it, before releasing it with a growl. She loves it when I bite her and be aggressive. "I knew you were checking the goods out," I tease. Leaning into her ear, I slide her hand down my stomach and into the top of my jeans. "Touch me then. Lick it. Bite it. Do whatever you want."

Leaning her head back, she lets out a small moan as I gently bite her neck, trailing my mouth down her body. "I want to," she breathes. "So damn bad, but . . ." She lets out a small scream and slaps my chest when I bite her harder. "We need to be careful, Stone. I thought we both agreed to put an end to this for now?"

Flipping her over, I spread her legs and place my body between them. "We have been," I say against her neck, before running my tongue up it. "Roommate fucking at its best, baby. The only strings will be when I tie you up. Now. Touch. Me."

Wrapping both of my hands in her hair, I lift my body, giving her just enough room to slip her hand where I want it.

We both want this right now and fuck me if I'm not going to just go with the flow and let it happen.

"You're so hard," she breathes, while rubbing me through my jeans. "This is going to be so hard. Why," she groans. "I don't want to follow the damn rules right now."

Pulling my bottom lip between my teeth, I push my jeans and boxer briefs down, freeing my erection for her. "Then don't."

Her breathing picks up as I yank my shirt over my head and toss it aside. "Stone . . ." She moans when I grip her thigh and press my hardness between her legs, poking her. "Stone." I poke her again to push her and work her up. "Fuck . . ." She moans.

Gripping her hair tighter, I slip my hand beneath her skirt, and push her panties to the side, exposing her slick pussy. "You wore panties this time," I point out, as I slide my finger over her wetness. "Is that your way of keeping in control when it comes to me?"

She nods her head and slides up the couch when I slip a finger inside. "Oh shit . . ." she moans out, while gripping the couch. "Wait."

Hearing the worry in her voice, I slide my finger out and suck it clean. "What's wrong, Sage? We've been playing by every rule since the beginning. Why are you so worried about breaking them once? One more time isn't going to make us fall in love or anything."

Breathing heavily, she places her hands on my chest to give herself more room. "Break them once and it leads to breaking them again and again." She stands up and fixes her skirt, looking regretful. "I can't take that chance with you and you know it. I should just go to bed while I'm still thinking straight." Her eyes look me over as I press down on my erection, feeling the blue balls creep in. "Stop being so sexy, Asshole," she says with a small smile. "Goodnight."

Respecting her wishes, I don't say a word as I watch her go to her room, shutting the door behind her.

"Fuck me . . . I'm going to need a cold shower."

I've never seen her so panicked before, then again, we've never come close to breaking the rules before. We've never had sex more than once in a month and now that we've agreed to stop messing around, we almost had sex for the second time this month.

Shutting off the lights after my fight-blue balls-shower, I crawl into bed and look over to see that it's past three in the morning. We're both tired and have been drinking for most of the night.

We just need to sleep it off.

If things are meant to happen between us, they will.

With time . . .

STONE

SWEAT'S DRIPPING DOWN MY SHIRTLESS body as I sit here in the dark, waiting for that private door to open so the show can begin.

It's been a long ass night and this is the last show I'm required to do, before I get my ass out of here for the night.

I've been dancing my dick off for seven hours straight, and no matter just how tired I truly am, nothing's going to stop me from showing this client a hot as fuck show.

When a client pays for a private show from me. They get the best. I put everything else behind me and dance until my body burns or my client's panties are soaking wet. Whichever comes first.

I'm not going to lie, I learned that from Slade in the beginning. Dude was a straight up beast and I knew I'd have to work hard to fill his shoes. Now with Slade, Hemy and Cale no longer dancing; *I'm* the one that Kash and Styx have to keep up with.

I grip the chair when I hear the door creak open. It's dark

enough in here that she can't see me yet, but I can see her as she nervously takes a seat on the couch below the small stage, waiting anxiously for the music to start.

When it does, the darkness on the stage dims enough for her to finally see me sitting here, half-naked, and ready to give her what she needs.

Something visual to get her off at night or maybe even here and now.

Moving my body to the slow rhythm, I slide my hand down my hard body, stopping on my cock. It's the quickest move to get her going and me out of here quickly.

Her eyes widen as I grab it and begin grinding my hips, slowly and torturously, while gripping myself as if I'm about to get off.

Hell . . . sometimes I do.

I don't miss it when she bites her bottom lip and lets out a small moan. It can be heard, even over the soft music.

Shit, I've barely even done anything yet, and she already looks as if she's ready to explode.

Her legs are now crossed and both of her hands are gripping the leather couch around her, her skirt riding up her legs as she grinds in her seat to get some friction.

Smirking, I stand from the chair and kick it out of the way, before sliding across the stage on my knees, until I'm sitting right in front of her.

Surprised, she throws both hands over her face, which I reach out and pull away, lowering them to the top of my jeans for her to unbutton for me.

Being this close, shows just how damn beautiful this woman is, but you can also see just how shy and nervous being here makes her.

A lot of women like her pay big money for these private

shows. The ones that are too scared to let anyone know that they're here in the first place. Strict family. Strict job. Or hell, maybe even a significant other.

That's not my job to worry about. My only concern is making sure that they leave here satisfied and dying to come back for more. And if they get off on it, then that's a damn bonus.

Pulling her chin up, so I can look her in the eyes, I sway my hips as her shaky hands work slowly to undo my jeans.

Breaking eye contact, I push her face down toward my hips, while grinding the air nice and fucking slow.

This causes her to get a little too excited, yanking my jeans down my thick legs as if she suddenly can't wait to get me in as little clothing as possible.

Being that close to my cock usually does the trick with these women, letting their inner freak come out.

Standing back up to my feet, I step the rest of the way out of my jeans and kick them to the side.

She gasps as her eyes lower to my white briefs, landing on my thick erection.

"Oh. My. God," she squeals.

I might sound like a cocky jerk, but I'm used to that reaction now. Although, it never seems to get old. I fucking love the look on their faces.

Smirking with confidence, I lower myself from the stage, straddling her lap.

My hands go straight for her hair, tangling up in the blonde strands as I grind against her, slow and hard, making sure that I dig into her body with each thrust.

It only takes a few seconds before her breathing picks up and I feel her jerk below me, letting out a long moan of satisfaction.

Once her orgasm stops, her eyes open back up and embarrassment crosses her pretty little features.

Taking a deep breath, she covers her face and shakes it back and forth. "I'm sorry," she says into her hands. "I'm so embarrassed."

Smiling, I remove her hands from her face. "You shouldn't be." I grab her chin. "I aim to please, baby girl."

She studies my face for a few seconds, before finally breaking into a smile. "So this happens a lot?"

Removing my other hand from her hair, I stand up and nod. "Every damn time. I have no problem being an orgasm donor. It's what my body was built for." I wink, causing her to laugh.

That's what I was going for. The last thing I want is for a client to leave, feeling bad or embarrassed because being here got them off instead of the privacy of their own home.

That's why Cale tested the private dances with me first, before letting the other guys start them. He knew with me, they'd leave here happy and satisfied. I have a way of making sure that happens.

Letting her eyes wander over my hard, sweaty body, she pulls a wad of cash from her bra and shoves it down the front of my briefs, making sure that her hand brushes the head of my dick. "Thank you. I needed that more than you know."

Looking pleased, she lets herself out of the room, leaving me alone to get dressed.

After I'm dressed and cleaned up, I stop up at the bar to grab a shot to help relax me after this long, hard night of having *everything* on my body pulled at.

Sara smiles at me and reaches for a shot glass. "Woah there! That was a fast show. Mr. Fucking Magic Dick."

Lifting a brow, I reach for the whiskey, slamming it back. The burn feels good right now, after such a long night here with the guys. It should help blur the memory of their dicks swinging.

"Yes, Ma'am." I slam the empty glass down and grab my

cock. "Nickname fits me to a T. It's a curse and a blessing." I release my junk and nod my head. "One more, babe."

I look around, searching for the security guard on duty, as she pours me one last shot. "Is Kage still here?"

"Yup." She rolls her eyes. "His big ass has been in the shower for the last thirty minutes, jerking off or some shit. You can get out of here. He'll stick around for me to close down."

"You sure?" I lift a brow, while tilting the second shot of whiskey back.

"Um . . . yes. I said so, didn't I?"

"Just double checking."

"Hey wait." I get ready to walk away, but Sara's voice stops me, causing me to turn back around. "You and Sage back at it yet or is she still teasing and torturing your smart aleck ass? I gave it six months and it's been seven. Just saying."

My cock instantly comes to attention at the sound of Sage's name. Damn that woman has my dick under some kind of spell.

"Apparently, my magic dick doesn't have a strong enough effect on her. She's the exception."

Winking, I walk away, with my mind stuck on Sage once again and the fact that we haven't touched each other since that night seven months ago.

You try living with a beautiful as fuck woman and keep your hands and dick to yourself.

Impossible as shit.

As hard as I try to get through one night around her without wanting to go back to our old ways, it's becoming impossible. The woman drives me mad.

And I fucking love the torture . . . I'll admit it.

As soon as I walk outside, the blonde from the private dance grabs ahold of my arm, pulling me around to the side of the building.

She doesn't bother speaking, going straight for my jeans and ripping them down my thick legs.

It's been a while since I've let this happen, but, I can't deny the fact that I need a little fucking action once in a while. As much as I want it with Sage . . . it's not going to happen.

A man has needs and I'm about to let this hot as fuck blonde satisfy them and try to not to feel guilty, knowing that I really have no reason to.

Sage hasn't asked about my sex life since we stopped being physical and I haven't asked her about hers.

Leaning against the building, I close my eyes and imagine Sage's mouth on my cock as blondie takes me into her mouth, sucking me hard.

I jump a little when she gets a little too excited, scraping her teeth over my shaft, while trying to fit most of my length in.

"Sorry," she mumbles around my cock.

Letting her know it's okay, I grip the top of her hair and begin thrusting my hips into her face.

Getting a little too excited myself, I push in a little too deep, causing her to gag on my length and dig her nails into my ass.

All it does is remind me that Sage has been the only one able to fully handle me sexually. It's like the girl was made for me.

How fucked up is that?

Gripping the blonde's hair, I pull her back so she can answer my question. "Can you handle my cock if I give you all of it?"

She nods her head and grips my ass tighter, letting me know that she's ready to try.

"I hope so," I whisper, *because I need to get off.*

Hoping that she's right, I turn her around and pull her head back as far as it can go, before shoving my cock into her mouth and fucking it hard and deep.

For some fucked up reason, seeing the shape of my thickness

in a girl's throat as I fuck her mouth, turns me on the most, usually getting the job done fast.

Within ten deep thrusts, I'm pulling out of the girl's mouth, releasing my load against the side of the building with a moan.

I feel the girl shove something into the back of my briefs. "Call me if you ever want to get together. *That* was me repaying you for the dance, but I'd like to do a lot more to you."

I don't even get a chance to turn around, before I hear the sound of the ground crunching as she walks away, leaving me alone to gather my shit.

She definitely wasn't as innocent as she looked, but nothing compared to Sage. No one ever is.

Fuck me . . .

chapter TWO

Sage

IT'S ONLY TWO IN THE afternoon and I already feel as if I've been here at the salon for an eight-hour shift. It's dragging so bad and I'm not liking it one bit.

"Oh come on," I groan out, as I throw myself down in the chair at Onyx's station. "Is time moving slower than usual today or is it just me? It's almost physically painful."

Smiling, Onyx grips my hair, yanking me back in the chair. "Shut up and let me color your hair to pass the time. I've been asking since last week to let me test something on you. You've been doing way too much griping the last few weeks. Would you just let Stone lay you already?"

"Shut up." I toss a comb at her. "If you're going to do my hair; do it in silence," I joke.

Aspen looks over at us from working on one of her clients, pointing her scissors at us as she talks. "One of you better keep your eye out for customers. We may be friends, and I love you to death, but take advantage of it and I'll kick your asses." She smiles slightly, but gives us a hard enough look to let us know she means it.

Two months ago, Aspen opened up her own Salon, *Raines' Salon*, and asked Onyx and myself to come work for her. Business started out slow at first, until the boys of *Walk Of Shame* started handing out business cards and sending the women here. Those boys ask you to do anything, you jump to it. At least these women did and not to mention that they tip well. A little something, they learned from going to *W.O.S.*

The business picked up like crazy after a couple of weeks, barely making it possible for us to keep up, thanks to the boys. Although, I do admit, every girl that walks through that damn door, I can't help but to wonder if Stone has been with since we stopped messing around.

I have to struggle between wanting to punch the bimbo in the face, and wanting to do my job, making her ass even prettier, when walking out that salon door.

Aspen has faith that I won't stab anyone with a stiletto, so I do my best. I just tell myself over and over again that I'm the one who stopped us from having sex that night.

When we first started messing around, it was easy, but after a year of occasionally letting loose with him and having the *best* sex of my damn life . . . let me tell you . . . that man can move his body; I started to want it more and more.

I could tell he did too.

"We've got your back, Sweets." Onyx winks. "I can multi-task. Just ask Hemy. He has plenty of stories."

"Fucking gross," I mumble, disgusted at the thought of the crazy shit I've heard about her and my brother. "Just don't mess my hair up or I'll have to chop yours off in your sleep. I'm not sure you'd pull the bald look off so well."

"I can pull anything off, Honey. Now shut it."

Closing my eyes, I try to relax and let Onyx take over. I know she'll do good, but since she's practically my older sister since marrying Hemy, I have to give her a hard time once in a while.

She's family and we treat each other that way. I'll never be able to repay her for bringing myself and Hemy back together. I owe her everything and I'm willing to give it too.

I honestly don't even know at this point how I went so long without my brother in my life. We went through so much shit as children and he was always there, until he wasn't.

I don't even remember how, but we got separated and I spent years missing him and trying to find him, until Onyx found me. She found me and brought my family back together.

I love her for that.

Onyx keeps pushing my head down, making sure that I look down at my boring ass lap for the whole hour that she's messing with my hair. Luckily, only two clients have come in that Onyx had to pull away from me to help and they were just quick trims.

Now my hair is dried and curled and the torture is done. It's not easy letting her push your head around for a whole hour, without wanting to slap her.

"Holy. Shit." Onyx pulls the purple cape off of me and her and Aspen look me over, making me feel nervous with their judging eyes on me. "I deserve a big tip for the miracle I worked on you, Honey."

"Wow," Aspen jumps in, while playing with my hair, lifting random pieces of it to look underneath the layers. "Maybe I should have you do mine next week."

Feeling anxious to see with my own eyes, I push them both out of the way and spin the chair around to look in the mirror.

"Holy. Fuck." My eyes widen as I check out the strands of turquoise, blue and purple, falling around my face. "This is definitely a new look. I have to give it to you . . . I look good," I say teasingly.

Between the new hair, lip ring and fresh tattoos, I almost feel like a whole new woman.

A wild one . . . and I like it. I feel sexy and playful, ready to get out and have fun for the first time in months, after spending my nights moping and trying to get myself off as good as Stone used to.

But as much as I like it, I can't help but to wonder what Stone would think, about both my new look and me wanting to go out and have fun.

It shouldn't bother me this much. I shouldn't be so worried about what he thinks. He's not my boyfriend and we both made it clear in the beginning that it was just for fun. He's just my roommate.

This is exactly what I *didn't* want us to turn into. He's grown on me big time and that's exactly why I've been avoiding anything about him that might turn me on more and change my mind. That's why I haven't even been to *W.O.S* in months now.

"I knew you'd like it," Onyx gloats.

I snap out of my thoughts and turn around to face my girls. "I do." I smile big and give her a quick hug, speaking next to her ear. "You're damn lucky I do too. I'll admit that you had me a bit scared with how confused you looked with the colors."

"Nah . . . I knew what I was doing. I just wanted to mess with you a bit." She winks and starts cleaning up the mess.

Aspen is still looking me over when I turn to face her. It's as if she can't get enough of how pretty it truly turned out. "I'm digging the new look on you. It seriously looks sexy. You going to visit Stone at work and see how long it takes for him to recognize you in the crowd?" She lifts a brow, pushing. "You can't avoid the club forever."

"Don't start this." Trying to avoid discussing Stone, I rush over to the counter when a client walks in, seeing it as my way to escape. "MINE."

"Whatever," Aspen mumbles from behind me, while motioning for her client to take a seat as she walks in right afterward. "We've got three more hours to bug you. Go right ahead."

"Seriously," I mumble under my breath, while checking out the brunette standing in front of me. She looks like a damn Barbie Doll, but with humongous tits.

"The boys sent me," she says with a huge ass smile, while placing down her twenty percent off coupon.

"Awesome." I grab the coupon and quickly check out the name of who gave it to her. I'm a little relieved to see Kash's name. "Follow me, babe."

Barbie girl decides to babble on about her experience at W.O.S over the past weekend, being sure to tell me every damn detail of how hot the boys were, and how sexy they moved their bodies, as if I don't already know.

That's the only *bad* and *good* thing about the boys sending them here. I feel as if there's a good chance that one of us girls would get the gossip if Stone is fucking these other women. The bad part of it is, that I hear so many stories and I can only handle so much and manage to keep my distance from there.

I hate myself for even wanting to know what goes on at the club, especially now that they have private rooms for dances.

From what I've heard, Stone's room is occupied the most and I have to say that I'm not surprised. He's very good at what he does.

By the time the salon is closed, Hemy is waiting outside for us, making sure that no one is lurking around the parking lot, even though it's only like six in the evening. It's not even dark, yet he worries so damn much.

Not much has changed there. He's a protector and always

has been.

As soon as we walk outside, Hemy instantly pulls Onyx into his big arms and kisses her along her neck, grinding his body into hers. He's always so quick to get dirty. "Damn, baby. Ready for a ride?" Continuing to kiss her neck, he cups her ass and lifts her up.

"I missed you. It's been a long ass day and I'm definitely ready for a ride," Onyx says against his lips, causing me to look over at Aspen and roll my eyes.

"Come on, guys. Seriously . . . you stopped in for lunch like five hours ago and fucked her in the back office. You act as if you haven't seen each other in weeks."

Releasing Onyx, Hemy walks over, draping his arm around me. From the look on his face, I know he's about to change the subject. "You going to come see dude tonight or what? Stone's somewhat of a miserable bastard without you around the club." He roughly kisses me on the side of the head. "Go watch him tonight so his pussy will stop hurting."

Grunting, I push my way out of Hemy's arms and begin digging through my purse for my keys. "Seriously? What is with it with everyone trying to get me to watch Stone dance? I'm trying to keep my thoughts in check when it comes to him. It's complicated."

"How?" he questions. "The dude is crazy over you and it's taken my ass over a year to accept that shit. Now what the hell am I supposed to give him a hard time about?"

Laughing, I begin backing away. "I'm sure you'll find other things. He's Stone . . ." I stop when his words really sink in. "And he's not crazy about me so don't say that again."

"Fine," Onyx cuts in. "Come to the club and watch the other boys tonight then. Hemy has to help Cale with some business crap in the office. Aspen or Riley can't make it. Don't make me sit there and drink alone. Just turn the other way when he's up."

"Maybe . . . we'll see. I want to write some tonight."

Saying bye to everyone, I hurry over to my truck and hop in, just ready to get home and take a short nap.

As much as I hate to admit it; I didn't sleep much last night. I ended up tossing and turning in bed, wondering what Stone was doing at work.

Maybe it's time I put on my big girl panties and go back into *Walk Of Shame* again.

Then maybe it will give me the confirmation that I need, to know that he's doing fine without me around and we can both move on.

There's plenty of other women there that would die to get Stone's attention.

Hopefully she can do more with it than I did . . .

chapter THREE

Sage

HEMY AND ONYX INISISTED ON following me to the *Walk Of Shame*, knowing damn well that I was hesitant and close to backing out of coming tonight.

They can't fool me, I know they're going to somehow try to get me into Stone's private room with him.

Not happening. I'm smart enough to know what will happen if he gets me alone.

I'll cave.

The jerks are teaming up on me, and I'm not so sure that I like it. Apparently, they've all grown fond of the idea of Stone and I possibly becoming a couple.

Maybe they see what we've been trying *not* to.

"Hey, Kage." I wink at the sexy security guard as he places his hand on the small of my back and guides me behind Hemy and Onyx, over to the VIP area.

"Keep winking at me and I might have to keep you to my-self now that Stone's out of the picture." He grabs a strand of my hair and smiles. "Very hot. I like my women wild looking. I bet we could have a lot of fun."

"Back the fuck off, Giant," Hemy growls out, while looking his six feet six frame up and down. "Don't you have a door to watch or some shit?"

Used to Hemy being a dick, Kage lifts a brow at him and smirks. "Can't help it if the *hottest* ladies in the club got my attention, Man."

"And I can't help it if I rip your motherfucking dick off."

"Hemy! Enough!" Onyx grabs Hemy by the back of the shirt, pulling him back to sit next to her on the couch. "Leave his dick alone. He's gonna need it tonight." She winks at Kage. "We got your back. Thank you, Sweetie."

I have to admit; being here and watching Hemy be all caveman and overprotective makes me laugh, reminding me of old times.

It used to drive me crazy when he treated Stone that way in the beginning and seeing him act this way now, shows me just how crazy his ass will be if I ever decide to go on a date.

Poor fucking guy . . .

"Can't take you anywhere, Big brother," I tease as I take my seat. "Now get us ladies some drinks and tell Sara hi for us, Mr. Rude."

His stripper instincts kick in, causing me to look anywhere *but* at him as he straddles Onyx's lap and grabs her face, making out with her.

When I turn back around, he stands up and licks his lips nice and slow. "I'll be right back. If any of the boys come over, tell them I said to fuck off."

"Seriously?" I scoot next to Onyx and link my arm with hers, as Hemy leaves us. "Is he ever going to give up and stop being a dick to every guy? He's so damn alpha."

Onyx shakes her head and smiles. "Nope . . . and I love it. Hemy will be Hemy and that's exactly why I keep his sexy ass around. That and because his . . ."

"No!" I yell. "I will slap you if you mention his . . ." I pretend to gag. "Don't make me slap your pretty little face. Please."

"Girls," Styx scoots his way in between us and hands us both a drink, before throwing an arm around each of us. "I took these from Hemy's ass while he was fighting a pack of rabid bitches off." He winks. "You're welcome."

Onyx sits up straight, her eyes wandering up to the bar. She's not beyond kicking some girl's ass for groping on her man. I've seen it and trust me, it's not pretty.

"They're gone now." He laughs. "And Hemy is getting new drinks and looking around as if he wants to rip someone's head off." Smirking, he stands up and brushes a hand through his blonde hair. "Don't tell his crazy ass that I'm the one that stole his drinks. I'm not trying to get my ass kicked tonight. This body has work to do. Later."

He quickly kisses us both on the cheek and rushes off to take the stage to get ready. The ladies love him with his tattoos, sexy pierced nipples and short, blonde beard. Not to mention his insanely beautiful blue eyes that are hard to not look at.

He's hot. What can I say? They all are.

Right as the music starts, Hemy heads back over from the bar, holding the replacement drinks. He growls when he looks down to see us both already holding drinks. "What the fuck? Whose ass do I need to kick? Was it Kash or Styx? Those sneaky fuckers."

We both shrug and laugh, pissing him off even more. It's fun to mess with him and see him get all worked up over the boys.

"I hate when you two team up on my ass. I give up before I get a nipple ripped off or some shit. You two are vicious." Tilting back his drink, he takes his seat on the other side of Onyx and wraps his arm around her, protectively.

We chat and drink for the next hour, making me anxious and curious about Stone.

He hasn't been seen in the whole time that we've been here. Makes me wonder if he's been giving private dances the whole time. The thought makes me sick to my stomach and I'm hating myself for it.

"You okay over there?"

"Huh?" I turn to the sound of Onyx's concerned voice. "What?"

"You've been staring off into space for the last twenty minutes, when you should be watching these boys on the stage and having some fun." She leans forward and begins looking around. "Is someone wondering about Stone? Is that it?"

I let out a fake laugh and cross my legs. "No. I was just thinking about the new book I'm working on and the asshole hero who won't stop pissing me off. Now shut up. Kash is on and his ass is looking extra sexy tonight."

Pretending to be into Kash's performance, I focus my attention on the stage and pull out some money to toss his way. He's insanely sexy, so it should be distracting me, but it's not enough to make me forget Stone and how badly I really want to watch him dance again.

Hemy disappeared twenty minutes ago to help Cale with some stuff in his office, leaving us girls here alone.

That's what he said at least, but I'm pretty sure Cale can handle it on his own.

I think he was just tired of watching the other boys strip since he can't do it himself anymore. Part of me thinks he misses it.

I definitely don't. *Vixen's* was fun while it lasted, but I definitely didn't see myself there long term.

Stripping is a big part of Hemy though. He had that when he didn't have Onyx and myself around. I think it kept him sane, while he was slowly losing himself to the darkness and pain.

My insides seem to melt and I find myself fighting to catch my breath at the sight of Stone across the room, leaning against the wall with his arms across his chest. How the hell does he manage to look so calm and cool standing there? It makes him extremely sexy and mysterious.

As much as I'm not wanting this kind of reaction, it's inevitable with Stone. He's always done this to me from the very first time I laid eyes on his painfully beautiful face.

"Fuck." I turn away and start fanning myself off in a panic. It suddenly feels extremely warm in here, knowing that he's about to work his body on stage soon.

"You okay, Woman?"

As hard as I fight not to look at him, my eyes find him again in the shadows, trying to stay clear of everyone so he can clear his head. He's wearing that black beanie of his, hoping that no one will spot him out until he's ready.

Well I will always be able to.

Onyx's eyes follow mine and she smiles, knowingly, once she sees what I'm secretly freaking out about.

Well at least I was trying to keep it a secret freak out . . . isn't working so well.

"You've got it bad for that boy. Just admit it and make it easier on all of us. You guys had fun together and that's how it should be."

Both of our eyes go back toward the stage once the music stops and Kash jumps down into the crowd, getting his moment that he loves so much. Being felt up at the end is his favorite part. Figures . . .

"Looks like your man's up next. Think you can handle his hotness?" She lifts a brow at me, while taking a sip of her drink. "That boys been working out some frustration or something. Damn . . . don't tell Hemy, but he's looking mighty fine. The last seven months have been good for his body."

We both watch as Stone walks away to get ready to make his way to the stage, most likely getting in position, waiting for his song to start.

Why the fuck does he have to be so sexy? Stupid jerk . . .

The room suddenly goes dark. I mean completely pitch black. I can't even see my hand in front of me.

A few women even scream, not expecting us all to be pooled in darkness. Hell, I almost screamed my damn self, surprised. I even spilled my drink some.

A small spotlight has us all staring at the stage as the DJ begins to play *In Chains* by Shamon's Harvest.

It's hard to make out at first, but at closer look, Stone is now down on his knees, shackled in chains.

Gripping the chains, he moves his hips in a way that is so damn sexy and hypnotizing that I accidently bite my bottom lip too hard, while watching him move.

"Fuck me . . ." I breathe. "Is it hot in here?" I tug at my blouse, not removing my eyes from his every move.

"Well damn. Look what you've done to him," Onyx breathes. "So much sin in that fine as hell body."

The more he moves around, the longer the chains get, allowing him to move closer to the edge of the stage, on his knees, while flawlessly fucking the stage at the same time.

Out of nowhere, surprising us all, water sprays all over the stage, soaking him and everyone in the front as he continues to fight the chains, his muscles flexing in the best ways possible to make him look even more irresistible.

He's wearing white boxer briefs. White! Wet and white! Dammit,

We're on the side of the stage and we even get a bit wet, and that's on top of the wetness between my damn legs now.

When the music speeds up, pumping us all up, he finally breaks free from the chains, causing my heart to race in excitement, as if I'm watching some intense movie or something, and the part I've been waiting for has finally just happened.

The women scream louder than I've ever heard, and wave their hands around, hoping that they'll choose them, as he walks to the edge of the stage and hops off.

I lose track of where he is, until I see a cute brunette, get lifted onto the stage, followed by him, jumping back up, sliding across the water on his knees to get to where she's standing.

Thrusting his hips, he slowly runs his hands down the front of his slick body, while standing up and removing his low hanging jeans.

He's wearing white boxer briefs. White! Wet and white! Dammit, Stone.

Running a hand through his dark, wet hair, he grabs the woman's hand with his free hand and runs it down his body, stopping at the top of his briefs.

I get nervous, thinking he's going to go lower, but he doesn't.

Biting his lip as the women scream, he thrusts his hips really fast, while pushing the woman down to her knees and grinding in her face.

All I can think about while his dick smacks her face, is how he used to grind his hips in my face, when giving me private dances and just how hot it made me.

Watching it happen with another woman just pisses me the fuck off.

I'm jealous. I'm actually jealous right now and this is not what I was hoping for.

Seeing this never used to bother me. Not when I was getting

it at home, but now . . .

"I want to cut that bitch," I mumble, surprised at my own words.

Onyx's eyes widen at my words. "Whoa there, killer. You act as if you haven't seen this a million times before."

I empty my glass and set it down. "Yeah, that was before, but I haven't seen it in a while. Maybe I'm just tired. It's been a long day."

I stand up and suck in a deep breath when Stone's eyes somehow find mine and lock on. The way he's looking at me, steals my damn breath away. There's so much intensity behind his eyes, knowing that I haven't been here in months and now here I am. I'm pretty sure he knows that I've been avoiding watching him dance.

Fuck . . . that look. I can't . . .

"I should go." I lean in and quickly kiss the side of her head. "Tell Hemy I said bye."

Knowing that she's going to try to leave with me, I push her back down when she attempts to stand. "I'm just going to bed so there's no reason for you to come with me. I'll see you tomorrow."

"Sage," she calls out when I turn to walk away. "Drive safe and call me if you need me."

"I always do."

I allow my eyes to land on the stage one last time, to see Stone standing still, with a small smirk on his lips. That smirk used to be my weak spot when we first met.

This pushes my ass to move faster and get myself out of here before I do something stupid, without thinking it through.

Coming here and watching him dance was a horrible idea . . .

STONE

I HAVEN'T STOPPED THINKING ABOUT Sage for one damn second, since watching her walk out that door, leaving me dazed on the stage.

She's been avoiding coming here since we stopped messing around seven months ago and the way she was watching me so intently, reminded me of when she used to want me.

Hell, maybe she still wants me to touch her just as badly as I still want to.

I barely snapped out of it, until Onyx jumped on the stage and threw her drink in my face, waking my ass up out of the trance I was in.

"You still over there thinking about Sage? Get a grip on your balls, Dude," Kash teases. "Don't be mad that she stayed for my show and yours ran her out." He cocks a brow, pissing my ass off even more.

"Fuck you!" I throw my sweaty ass, soaked briefs at his face and laugh when he freaks out.

"Dude! Your balls were just in these. What the fuck."

"Next time it will *be* my balls slapping your pretty face, Asshole."

"I'm out, Dicks. Got a kinky ass woman waiting outside my house. If you get some pictures from me, open with caution, Fuckers." Styx throws his bag over his shoulder and slaps us both upside the head, before taking off.

Asshole's lucky, I don't feel like wasting my energy on his ass. Fuck, I don't feel like wasting it on anyone, but Sage. I don't need sleep. I'd spend the whole night pleasuring her if I got the chance to again.

I wanted nothing more than to run off the stage and dance for her, but I was worried she might get pissed and the last thing I want is to embarrass her by putting her on the spot.

Well fuck me . . .

Why was she even here tonight after so long? If it was for one of these other assholes, I won't hesitate to fuck them up. None of them are good enough for her and none of them will take care of her like I would if given the chance.

"Think Sage would let me come over tonight?" Kash teases.

"Hell no, Fucker. I'm getting out of here before I kick your ass. I'm not in the mood so don't test me tonight."

Smirking, he throws his hands up and backs away to the shower. "It's all good. My hand's been good to me."

"I bet," I mumble, once I'm alone. "Mine too. Mine fucking too."

I finish gathering up my shit, before going to find Cale in his office, hoping that Hemy is still here so I can ask about Sage.

He's not.

Cale stands from his chair and starts grabbing for his shit. "You good?" he questions. "You look a little stressed."

Raking my hands through my wet hair, I let out a breath of

frustration. "You saw who was here tonight," I point out. "Did Hemy tell you why?"

He walks out the door, with me following behind. "Onyx made her come, Man. She didn't want to drink alone."

"Yeah," I say. "I figured she wasn't here to see me or those other dicks. Thanks, Man, I'll see you later."

"Not a problem, Man. Take it easy and I'll see you later. Try not to stress over her too much. Things will work out if they're meant to."

"You're probably right," I say mostly to myself, before we both take off for the night.

———————

BY THE TIME I GET home, the house is dark and Sage is in her room, asleep.

Unable to sleep myself, I find myself in the shower at five in the damn morning, jerking my shit to thoughts of Sage's sexy as sin body, remembering every last detail of how her body felt against mine.

It didn't help that she came into the club tonight somehow looking even sexier than usual, sporting a new hair style. With her wild hair, fresh tattoos and lip ring . . . fuck me. She looks wild and sexy as fuck.

What I wouldn't do to suck that piercing into my mouth and nibble it. Hell . . . I want to feel it on my dick.

Closing my eyes, thoughts of her take control of me.

The curve of her hips.

Fuck yes.

The fullness of her beautiful breasts.

Fuck me.

The way her tight little pussy hugged my cock so perfectly.

Fuck . . . so damn perfect.

Gripping the shower wall, my hold on my shaft tightens and my strokes speed up, bringing me so close to losing my shit, that I almost can't handle it.

A few more long, hard strokes and I'm growling out my pleasure, while shooting my hot cum down the drain, pretending it was Sage's plump ass. How I'd love to see my release drip down her sexy little asshole.

"Oh. Fuuuuck!"

Standing in the warm shower, I close my eyes harder, while fighting to catch my breath.

That woman does something to me that I can't fight.

And it turns me on like nothing else . . .

AFTER MY SHOWER, I SOMEHOW managed to pass out and not wake up until close to noon.

The first thing I did when getting out of bed this afternoon, was start thinking about how Sage was at the club last night, watching me.

She looked like she was sweating from watching me. I could tell, even in the darkened room.

"Fuck this." I'm tired of this new arrangement and tired of pretending as if I don't want her.

I've stepped back for seven months now and have respected the fact that we weren't going to be physical anymore, but I want more with her and I'm tired of holding back.

I'm about to refresh her damn memory of me and remind her of what she's missing.

When she first moved here to Chicago, over a year ago, she couldn't stay away from me, despite her brother giving us a hard time for messing around.

We had fun. We were good with each other . . . for each

other, until she got scared and decided we were done being friends with benefits. I wasn't ready to stop, but kept my mouth closed out of respect.

I want to show her that not everyone in her life will disappear. Not everyone will hurt her and abandon her like her parents did. Especially me.

I want to make her mine and I'm not stopping until I do. The old Stone charm is coming out to play . . .

chapter FIVE

Sage

THERE'S NOTHING I HATE MORE than trying to avoid Stone while being in the same house, but after going to the club last night, I haven't been able to stop thinking sexual thoughts about him.

I thought I could handle living with him and not wanting more with him, but it's becoming harder and harder with each day.

The truth is, I never wanted to stop in the first place, but I was starting to depend on him being there for me.

The feeling scared me, because after my parents abandoned us when I was a child and Hemy and I got separated; alone was all I had.

There was never anyone that I had to worry about losing, because I ended up with a family that didn't even know I existed. They were just in it for the money and couldn't give a shit whether I lived or died.

There was no one for me to lose. No one that had the power

to hurt me. Hemy was already gone and he was the only person who ever mattered to me.

Then the day that Onyx found me working in that coffee shop, she became my friend. She was the first person I had let in since losing my brother.

Stone was the second and I didn't even mean to let him in. The fucker charmed his way in and got stuck.

Distancing myself was the only thing I could do to protect myself from falling and getting hurt and the more nights we spent having fun, flirting and having sex, the more I started to feel for him and fear him disappearing too.

I knew I shouldn't have gone to *W.O.S* last night. One reminder at what he could do with his body and I was completely done for. If I even give him the chance to talk to me right now; I'm utterly screwed.

It's my day off and I plan on spending it in my room, finishing up this damn book and keeping my mind *far* away from Stone.

Stone doesn't exist . . .

"Stone doesn't exist," I say out loud this time. "And neither does his humongous dick."

"Sure I do, Honey and my humongous cock definitely exists as well."

Scared shitless, I practically jump out of my chair, while spinning around to the sound of Stone's voice.

"You fucker!" I suck in a deep breath at the sight of Stone gripping the doorframe. *Those muscles don't exist. That body. That bulge . . .*"What are you doing in here? Ever heard of knocking. Jeez, Stone."

A smirk crosses his sexy as sin face. "Since when have I ever knocked?"

Closing down my laptop, my eyes follow Stone's every move

as he walks into the room and takes a seat at the edge of my desk.

I can't seem to keep my eyes off of his thick, muscled thighs. I always loved that about him. So much power in them.

"Well it's always a nice gesture. I was writing."

My heart races like crazy as my eyes wander over his body, stopping on his smooth lips, waiting for him to say something. Anything.

Why does my body have to react this way to him? Why does it have to want him so badly?

"You got me thinking last night." He scoots across the desk, until he's right in front of me, pulling my chair closer, until I'm between his legs. "About how much you used to love me dancing for you."

My breath escapes me when Stone's hands come around to grip my hair and he slowly lowers his body into the armless chair and down to straddle my lap.

His warm breath tickles my ear as he leans in close, knowing what his closeness will do to me. "It's been a while, but I bet me being this close still affects you."

Letting loose for a moment, I wrap my arms around his firm body and moan when he begins grinding in my lap. "No," I breathe.

He runs his lips up my neck, stopping below my ear. "No, it doesn't still affect you?" Pulling my hand from around him, he places it on his chest and slowly starts moving it down his hard body.

"Yes," I breathe. "I mean no." Trying to keep in control, I yank my hand away from his body, before I can cave in. "Let's not do this, Stone."

"Why?" he whispers, while wrapping his hand in my hair. "Remind you of good times? Of the many ways my body made you come?"

"You know it does, Jerk." I push his rock hard chest, until he finally backs away from me. "It's not like I've forgotten just because we haven't been physical in months. What's gotten into you?"

He must notice me checking his chest out, because a cocky smirk appears on his face. "Take my shirt off if you want. I'll let you lick it."

I clear my throat and stop gawking at his body, before he decides to take it as an invite back into my panties. "You're a pain in my ass," I say with a small smile. "Do you know that?"

"I want to *fuck* you," he growls out, surprising me. "This new hair. Fuck me, Sage. There's nothing you can do to make me not want you as much. You get sexier every damn time I lay eyes on you."

I can't deny the way my body gets all happy and giddy from his words. Him not being afraid to say what's on his mind always turned me the hell on.

"Stone . . ." I warn. "Why are you doing this?"

"I'm thinking about running my tongue over every inch of your body right now. Remember how much you loved my tongue on you?"

He runs his tongue over his bottom lip and I instantly get wet, at just the memory of how good it used to make me feel.

The boy had a magic tongue and a magic dick and I miss them both.

Shit . . . he needs to get out of here. Now!

"Oh I remember. Trust me, but I'm trying not to. Especially right now so I can work. Please, let's not bring up the past. I won't be able to concentrate."

"You missed the last part of my dance last night. Come to my private room tonight at eleven and let me make up for it. Just one dance is all I'm asking." He laces his hands behind my neck like old times and leans in to press a kiss right beside my lips. "One night to be in charge and pleasure you without sex. Just give me that. You look like you need release and I want to help you with that. Nothing more."

Exhaling, I close my eyes and run my hands over my face as Stone walks out of my room and leaves.

I don't waste any time jumping out of my chair and locking the door behind him so he can't distract me anymore.

It's bad enough that my minds been on him since last night, but now . . . *damn him.*

Now he's asking me to let him give me a private dance. Does he realize what that's going to do to me?

Yes, I got off on watching his body and yes I do need it. He wasn't wrong about that.

But he wasn't supposed to notice.

Fuck my life . . .

Letting my frustration out on paper, I pull up my work in progress and end up getting in a total of seven thousand words in just under three hours. Only two thousand or so more to go and it's done. My third book.

My hero somehow ended up with a lot of Stone's qualities. A cocky, smart ass, sex maniac with a magic dick.

Of course he would find a way to take over my book too. That ass.

Riley called me about an hour ago, asking me to come over and spend some time with her and precious little baby, Haven, so here I am.

She's two weeks today and so damn cute that I swear I could just die.

Cale's at *W.O.S* for the next hour so I figured it would be nice to get some girl time in and see what she has to say about my situation with Stone.

"So what should I do?"

"I'm sorry. What?" Riley looks up from baby Haven in her arms. "She's very cute and distracting," she says in a baby voice. "Repeat that, please."

"Stone. He asked me to come see him tonight and . . ." I get distracted myself and completely lose track of what I'm saying when Haven smiles over at me. "How can something be so damn cute," I coo. "Look at you. Look at you so cute with your precious little nose and big eyes."

Riley laughs at me when I shake my head. "Told you she's distracting."

"Okay, seriously this time." I shield my face from looking at Haven, before she can work her baby voodoo on me again and mess up my thoughts. "Should I go tonight? He wants to dance for me?"

Riley lifts her eyebrows suggestively. "If you want to let that boy back between your legs. Cause' you know that's going to happen." She pauses to reach for Haven's bottle when she begins fussing. "There's no way that I could watch Cale strip for me without wanting him between my legs afterward. Doesn't matter if I haven't seen him dance in six months or a whole year. We've already tasted the goods, sweetie and we'll always want more. Those boys were trained to make us sweat."

"Tell me about it," I mutter. "That's what I'm afraid of. I thought we were done with that stuff."

"Do you want to see Stone dance? Do you miss how it made you feel? If it does then go. Live a little. Have some fun while you're still young."

I focus on my phone when a text comes through from Stone. Before even opening it, my heart already speeds up with excitement.

Stone: Wear that skirt I like. No fucking panties. Like old times.

My heart speeds up even more after reading it and my thoughts fill with the many times that I've worn that skirt for him, causing my pussy to clench with excitement.

I'm so hot just thinking about him and what he can do to my body, that I can barely handle it.

That's my damn answer.

"I guess I do. More than I should. Dammit."

Saying goodbye to Riley and the baby, I

shove my phone into my purse and jump into my truck, driving off.

I know without a doubt that by showing up tonight; I'm giving him the okay to pleasure me how he wants.

It's taken me over seven months to be okay with him not touching me anymore.

Do I really want to jump back on his sexual adventure, knowing where it will possibly lead?

I've only got three hours to figure it out and my body is begging me to say yes.

Damn you, Stone . . .

STONE

TEN MINUTES 'TIL ELEVEN AND no sign of Sage yet. I almost let disappointment set in until I remind myself that I'm taking charge of tonight. It's happening whether it's here at *W.O.S* or back home in Sage's room.

I'm not giving up until I get her where I want her, and that's back to wanting me just as much as I want her.

I'm just getting dressed after my quick shower, when Styx walks out from the other shower, naked and dripping wet.

"Ever heard of a towel, Dipshit?"

He runs a hand through his thick, wet hair and shrugs, before fingering his short beard. "Never use them. You haven't figured that shit out by now?"

I toss my dirty towel at him just to piss him off. "That's why I asked, Fucker."

Standing up, I get ready to pull my shirt on, when the door opens and Kash pokes his head in. "Fuck me . . . when did Sage get so sexy?"

Out of instinct, I stiffen up, ready to kick his ass, but quickly remind myself that she showed up after all. "Touch her and I'll rip your dick off, Pretty boy."

"Hey, Man. I can't help it if I noticed how sexy she looks tonight in the skirt she's wearing. Holy fuck . . . my cock got hard." He steps into the room and points at his crotch. "It still hasn't gone down."

She wore the skirt like I asked. Well . . . hell.

"Yeah, well you better get your cock out of my way if you want to keep that shit working."

Grinning, he steps away from the door when I head toward it. "Hey. It's not my dick you have to worry about. She was with Lane when I saw her."

"Fucking shit."

I swear the damn security team here is almost worse than us strippers when it comes to the women.

I've caught Kage, Lane and even Kass getting their fair share of blowjobs and pussy in empty rooms when Cale isn't around watching our asses.

Hell, I've been guilty of that shit too, but those fuckers are bad. Especially Lane.

By the time I fight my way through the crowd and get to Lane; Sage is gone.

"Where is she, Man?"

Lane gives me a look as if I'm crazy or some shit. "Who? There's about a hundred females here tonight."

"Sage. Did she leave?"

He smiles. "I should've known she was here to see your ass." He points toward the back where the private rooms are. "She headed that way."

Feeling confident, I raise a brow. "I have a show to put on and it might take a while. Tell Kass to keep everyone away from my room. No private shows. Tell him to send them to Styx or Kash if they ask for me."

"I'm sure I can keep them busy," he says cockily. "No worries."

Not wanting to keep Sage waiting for too long, I quickly head through the private door to my room, that's just for the dancers, and slip into a suit and suspenders, remembering just how hot she got the first time I stripped out of a suit for her.

Women love my ass in a suit and tie. Add some suspenders and it's a done deal.

Getting into position on the stage, I set my eyes on Sage sitting on the couch, waiting for the music to start.

I just hope she's ready to go back to the beginning . . . back to when she couldn't resist my ass.

Sage

SITTING HERE WAITING ON STONE, I can't help but to wonder what I'm getting myself into.

I struggled for hours, trying to decide whether or not I should just stay home and pretend that he never barged into my room, leaving my body aching for his touch when he left.

I couldn't do it.

He's the only thing I've been able to think about since and it's been driving me crazy. As hard as I fight it, I can't help but to adore everything about Stone.

Oui by Jeremih begins playing over the speakers, letting me know that he's now on the darkened stage, ready to do what he does best.

Getting comfortable, I lean back and cross my legs, keeping my eyes on the small stage as it lights up just enough for me to see him standing there in a suit.

Holy. Shit.

Stone in a suit has to be about the sexiest thing on this earth and he knows it.

His body begins moving to the rhythm of the music, his hands rubbing seductively down his chest, landing on his crotch as he thrusts. The way his hips move instantly gets me sweating.

Biting his bottom lip, he hops off the stage and picks me up, chair and all, and begins walking back up to the stage to set me down in the middle.

Without missing a beat, he grabs the top of my chair tilting me back until he's standing above my face. Then he begins fucking the air so damn perfectly that I bite my lip so hard that I draw blood.

Stone is good with his body. Sometimes I think too damn good. When that music starts; there's no stopping him until you're completely fucking wet.

Placing me back upright, he stands up and his hands begin working on the buttons of his black, fitted button down.

I find myself watching in anticipation, waiting to see his body as if it were the first time. And holy shit is it exciting, especially since he's practically treating me like a stranger at the moment. It makes it feel more like the first time.

Slowly thrusting his hips, he breaks the bottom two buttons open on his shirt, pulling it off, so that he's now only in a pair of black slacks a tie and suspenders.

Oh my god . . . is he gorgeous.

His hands go up to undo his tie, before he slips it from around his neck.

Smirking cockily, he wraps it behind my neck and scoots my

chair across the slippery stage, until he's straddling my lap and grinding on me.

Feeling anxious to touch him, I slide my finger under a strap of his suspenders and snap it.

With force, he captures both of my hands and pulls them behind me in the chair, before running his tongue up my neck, stopping under my ear. "No touching unless I say so."

I let out a surprised gasp as he wraps his tie around my wrists and securely ties it where he knows there's no way I'm getting out. Panic sets in a little because Stone's never been this rough before. It's new and exciting, yet I can't help but to feel anxious awaiting his next move.

My insides clench as I watch him moving his body of pure tattooed muscle, while working on the straps of his suspenders.

"Oh. My. God," I whisper.

Stone is good. Too damn good and I'm not sure whether to love him for this hot show he's putting on or hate him for making my body crave for him once again.

Licking his hand, he runs it down his hard body and into his pants, thrusting the air three times in a way that's so seductive that I gasp for air. My eyes trail down to where his hand is moving, to see him stroking his thickness beneath the fabric.

It doesn't take much to see that he's not wearing anything beneath those suit pants and I'll admit that I want nothing more than for him to lose them.

With his free hand, he undoes the button and zipper, giving me a better view of him slowly stroking his cock. The sight has my pussy clenching and my whole body aching to touch him. Just one feel of what I used to get.

He's not going to let me. He's doing this on purpose to torture me and he's doing a damn good job at it.

Before I know it, he's done stroking himself for me and is

slowly lowering me out of the chair to the ground, looking down at me and biting his lip as he walks around me.

He waits until the right moment of the song, before straddling me, working his body over mine until he's above my face.

Going with the beat of the music, he sways and grinds his hips above my face as if fucking it nice and slow. His hard cock is on display above my face and I'm fighting with everything in me not to brush my tongue along every hard inch of it and own it.

It's so insanely hot having him so close, but untouchable. I let out a small moan as he grips my hair and moves more aggressively above me, getting closer to my mouth, but still just out of reach.

Where the hell did he learn to move this way? So damn sinful.

Out of nowhere, he stands and flips me over, pulling my ass up until it's in the air and my face is pressed against the ground.

He walks around me as if admiring my form, before stopping in front of me and groping his thick erection, letting it hang out of his pants, completely.

Breathing heavily, I watch him, wanting nothing more than for him to come in front of me as he brushes his pre-cum over the head of his dick and moans.

Biting his bottom lip, he walks around me again, before dropping to his knees behind me, grabbing my hips and thrusting against my ass to the music.

I find myself gripping at the stage and moaning from release at the feel his dick rubbing me through my thin panties. It's so damn hard and big, rubbing me in the right damn spot, repeatedly and in consistent thrusts.

My body jerks below him, trying to come down from its high, until he grabs my neck and pulls me back, pressing his lips below my ear.

"Oh yea, ah yea, ah ah yea," he sings seductively. "Hey. There's no we without you and I."

Oh hell . . . he has a sexy voice.

The music stops and I find myself breathing so damn hard that I'm almost embarrassed that he could do this to me after so long and with me tied up.

Now that the room is silent, all I can hear is the sound of Stone's heavy breathing against my ear. "Fuck me, you wore the skirt." His hand reaches beneath my skirt to skim my panty line. "You were smart wearing these," he whispers.

"Yeah," I breathe. "I have to be around you, Stone. You're slick. I haven't forgotten."

A knock sounds at the door, causing Stone to groan into my ear and release my hair to untie my hands.

That's all it takes for me to snap out of Stoneland and gather my thoughts. "I should go so you can work. Thanks for the dance." I free myself from his hold and get back to my feet, while I still have my thoughts in check. "It was good." I smile. "Really good, but we still need to go back to how things have been. It's been working for us and I don't want to mess that up."

I make the mistake of looking back at him to see him on his knees, gripping his sweaty hair in frustration. He looks pained and disappointed.

I've never seen this kind of emotion from him. He's always the funny, care free guy. Seeing him in this light makes my heart stop, but I try not to let it confuse me even more.

The knocking starts up again. "Give me a fucking minute," he growls out.

Standing to his feet, he walks over to me and grips the bottom of my hair. "I'm not that easy to get rid of, Sage. I have lots of things I want to do to your beautiful body. Lots of things I haven't shown you yet." He gently places a kiss beside my lips, before fixing his pants, smirking and walking out the door.

"What the hell," I breathe in a panic. "What is he doing to me?"

I stay in Stone's room for a good ten minutes, pulling myself back together before exiting and jumping in surprise, when Kage is waiting outside.

"Kage!" I laugh as he smiles at me. "What are you doing?"

He wraps his huge arm around me. "Stone's ass asked me to keep my eye on you. He got called back to do a short show for a bachelorette party in the back room and couldn't get out of it."

My eyes travel over to the back room when I hear a few screams of excitement. "Looks like someone has a busy night."

Kage lifts a brow. "I'm free in ten."

Smiling, I place my hand on Kage's hard stomach. "Thanks, Big guy, but I have to be up early."

He winks. "Your loss."

"I'll be sure to cry myself to sleep tonight."

Pulling my hand away, I blow him a kiss and back away. "Goodnight, Giant."

As soon as I get out to my truck, my mind drifts off to Stone and how badly I need to pleasure myself after what he just did to me, and I have a feeling it will be to thoughts of him and all of the things he's done to me in the past.

This is going to be a long night . . .

SEVEN

STONE

I'M SITTING OUTSIDE SLADE'S HOUSE, smiling to myself as I remember the way Sage's body reacted to me last night. Fuck me, she was so wet for me.

She may be fighting hard to keep me out, but she still wants me and last night proved it just by her showing up in the first place.

It took everything in me not to rip her wet panties off and sink so deep between her legs that she'd feel me inside her for days.

It's too soon, so I settled with getting her off the only way I knew she'd let me at that point.

Tonight is my night off and I plan to be wherever she's going to be. I haven't seen her all day since she's been working, but I plan to make tonight count.

Stone: What are you doing tonight?

A few minutes later, my phone vibrates in my hand with a

response from Sage.

> *Sage: I have plans, big guy, and not with you.*

> *Stone: You sure about that?*

> *Sage: I'm pretty positive you don't have a vagina . . . so yes.*

> *Stone: No . . . but I'd like to pound yours. Now tell me where.*

> *Sage: Damn you Stone . . . Your fucking mouth.*

> *Stone: I'll put it anywhere you want.*

> *Sage: . . . I bet you will, big guy. ;) Now bye.*

She loves my mouth and I know without a doubt that she's now picturing it all over her body and remembering all of the ways I've tasted her.

That's all I need. Is to be on her mind and last night gave me the opportunity that I needed.

Jumping out of my jeep, I jog up to Slade and Aspen's door to find that it's locked, before running around to the back and letting myself in. They always keep the back unlocked.

Stepping into the kitchen, I go to open the fridge and stop when I hear moaning and what sounds like spanking coming from the living room.

Smirking, I open a beer and toss the lid aside before going to stand in the doorway.

All I see is Slade's naked ass pounding away as if he hasn't gotten laid in weeks.

"Where's the popcorn, Dude?"

Growling, Slade thrusts into Aspen one last time, before turning to look at me. "What is with you fuckers never knocking?"

Covered up, Aspen sits up from the couch and peers over the top. "Don't you guys ever get tired of walking in on us?"

I tilt back my beer and smile. "The question is . . . don't *you* guys get tired of us walking in on you? It's called locks, but you always leave the back door open. You enjoy it . . . admit it."

Slade stands up completely naked and gives me a dirty look while pulling his briefs up. "You're early, Dick. I just walked in the door thirty minutes ago. Can't a guy please his wife and shower after work in peace before dealing with your ass?"

"Now that's asking a lot." I raise a brow just to annoy him more. "How are things at the office going, Suit? I bet it's exciting as shit sitting behind a desk all day."

"It's more relaxing than shaking my cock all day, Fucker. How's yours now that Sage has your balls? Is it holding up on its own?"

"Nothing can keep my shit down, Man." I smirk and grab my crotch. "I've got a magic dick is what I've been told."

"Yeah, well tell your magic dick to toss me a beer."

Aspen stands up, pulling the blanket with her. "I'll be upstairs showering and finishing what you interrupted so thanks for that, Stone."

I smile against my beer. "Hey, no one said you had to stop. It's not as if I've never seen it before."

Aspen's face turns red. "Well I think you've seen it enough." She walks over to kiss Slade on the neck. "I'll be waiting for you upstairs."

Growling, Slade grabs Aspen's ass through the blanket and slaps it as she walks away.

Laughing, I toss Slade a beer and he catches it, quickly popping the top off. "So how did things go last night? Sage show up?"

"Yup." I pull out a bar stool and take a seat. "She's still

pushing my ass away." I tilt back my beer. "But at least she came."

He smiles and takes a swig of his beer. "It's been what . . . six or seven months since she's watched your annoying ass dance. Good shit. So you're going all in this time? You really want more?"

"Yeah." I set my beer down and watch as he searches through the fridge. "I only held back the first time because I was respecting the fact that she wanted nothing more than to mess around. I did things her way and now I'm doing them mine. We were roommates for a whole damn year, messing around when she wanted to. I want more, Man. I know she's scared, but I won't hurt her."

He pulls out some lunchmeat and begins making a sandwich. "You sure about that?"

"Hell yeah," I say without hesitation. "I may have been pushed around and kicked in the past, but I'm not scared of love, Man. Not like her. It's the opposite for me. I want it."

He nods his head and tosses some bread my way for my own sandwich. "You better hope so. If you hurt Sage; Hemy will break your ass in two."

I think about it for a second and my answer remains the same. She's the only thing I've been able to think about since laying eyes on her. She means something to me and I want to find out just how much.

"Positive." I throw some turkey and mustard on my bread, before taking a huge bite. "I just need her to spend some time with me out of the house so she can see how much fun we used to have."

Slade watches me for a few seconds, before speaking again. "Make sure your ass is at *Fortunes* tonight then. She asked Aspen to come out with her and Jade for a few drinks around nine."

"No shit." Smiling, I stand up and look at the clock. It's a quarter to seven. "You and Aspen going?"

He shakes his head. "Nah, Aspen's had a long week. We're staying in."

"Looks like Kash's ass better prepare to come out then." I shove the last bite of sandwich in my mouth, before finishing off my beer and tossing it in the trash. "You've just made my night a hell of a lot better. I need to get my ass home and change."

"Anything to get you out of my house, Fucker. My woman is waiting upstairs for me to finish what you interrupted." He tosses his empty beer in the trash. "Lock the back door on the way out."

With that, he walks away, leaving me alone in his kitchen.

I quickly clean up the mess we made and then let myself out the back, locking the door behind me.

Once back in my jeep, I send Kash a quick text, letting him know that he's coming out tonight.

He responds within a few seconds.

Kash: I'm down.

I knew he would be and I need someone to keep Jade busy so I can get close to Sage tonight.

As close as she will allow me . . .

chapter EIGHT

Sage

JADE HAS BEEN IN HER room for the last hour finishing up her makeup, so I've been watching her little brother, Jake, and one of his friends play pool.

Her brother just turned eighteen two days ago and seems to think that now that he's of age, that I'm going to give him a shot and let him take me home to his parents' basement.

I don't think he realizes how creepy that sounds.

The kid says he has huge plans for me and that his parents hardly ever come down to the basement.

Apparently, his friend seems to get a kick out of him trying and being turned down and put in his place by me, because he's been laughing his ass off for the last hour.

"You know . . ." Jake pauses to take his shot and misses. "I just upgraded to a queen-sized bed, Baby. That means it's fit for a queen. My queen."

Laughing, I about spit my beer out. "I'm sorry, but I only lay with a king, Kid. Let me know when you get your next upgrade."

"Oh damn." His friend covers his mouth with his fist and busts out in laughter.

"Really, Jake?" Jade laughs from the doorway. "You definitely got your game from uncle Frank and trust me, it's not strong, Kid."

Jake rolls his eyes. "Stop calling me kid. Did you miss the part where I turned eighteen? Dammit, Jade. You're always trying to embarrass me and crap."

Smiling, she grabs her brother's chin and starts talking in baby talk about how cute and adorable he is.

This causes him to turn red with embarrassment and toss his cue stick down. "Dude . . . let's get out of here, Myles, while I still have some dignity left."

"Bye, Cutie," I tease. "Don't forget to call me when you get an upgrade." I wink, causing him to smirk and smooth out his shirt.

"It's the shirt, right?" He nudges his friend. "Told you she'd dig the shirt."

Jade grabs both of the boys and begins pushing them through the house. "Time to leave. Tell mom I'll call her tomorrow."

Myles stops to check Jade out in her black skinny jeans and teal blouse. "I turn eighteen in three months." He licks his lips. "Just sayin'."

"Out!" She points. "Jake, don't forget your weird little sidekick."

We both look at each other and laugh as the boys argue their way out the front door about who's game needs the most work.

"Well . . . that was interesting." Jade smiles. "You ready to go out and see some *real* men now? I just heard that the after party for the MMA fights from tonight is going to be at *Fortunes*. Plenty of hard powerful, hot men to choose from."

The thought of these MMA fighters being at the bar tonight is sort of exciting, but I can't help but to think of the fact that Stone is built the same way, but even better than most of these fighters.

When I think *hard, powerful and hot* . . . I think Stone.

His body is hard and powerful and he's definitely got to be the hottest guy I've ever laid eyes on.

Trying not to fall for him has been harder than I imagined. Especially when he opens his sexy mouth, telling me what he wants without holding back.

He's gone months being quiet, but I have a feeling that's about to change.

"Let's go." Shaking my head of thoughts of Stone, I follow Jade outside to her jeep.

Fortunes is already busy by the time we get there. My guess is that the fights are over and everyone is gathering around to drink with their favorite fighters.

The crowd is already rowdy from drinking and watching the fights so the bar is so loud that you have to practically scream to hear each other.

"We'll take two beers," Jade yells to the bartender, while holding up two fingers for her to see.

"Holy shit," I say next to Jade's ear as she hands me a beer. "You can't even move in this place tonight. Is it always this way after a fight? It's so hot in here and smells like sweat."

"Always, Honey. You need to get out more," she yells. "And tell me about it. They need to crank up the air with all of these sweaty men in here."

Holding onto Jade's arm, I pull her through the crowd until I spot the last empty table in the whole bar.

It just so happens to be next to the table that a few fighters have just arrived at. The whole table is screaming and congratulating the guys on their wins, while passing cans of beer around.

"See that guy with the black shirt?" Jade asks, while pointing to the hot blonde with bulging muscles. I nod my head. "That's Knight Stevens. He was the main event at the fights down the street. Looks like he won."

Within seconds, trays full of shot glasses arrive at their table, most of them being passed over to this Knight guy as he continuously slams them back, accepting them all.

I tilt back my beer while watching him. "He's a fucking trooper. Holy shit, I'd be puking my ass off by now."

"Tell me about it. I love a man that can handle his liquor." She takes a swig of her beer. "He's single too. Maybe we should go over and congratulate him."

This Knight guy must catch us looking at him and talking, because his eyes land on us and stay there as he tilts back one last shot.

Winking, he nods his head and grabs two shot glasses, before heading over to our table. He sets the shot glasses down, before eyeing us both over like he's ready to take us to his hotel room and show us a good time. "Drink up, ladies. Shots are on my table."

Jade grabs a shot and nudges me when I don't make a move to grab one. "Thanks. Can't refuse a drink from the champion." She waits for me to grab mine, before clinking her glass against mine and downing it at the same time that I do mine.

Satisfied, Knight helps us both to our feet, before grabbing our table and pushing it against his. "The prettiest girls here and you guys are sitting alone. I won't have that shit. You're with me now." He winks, while getting pulled away by one of his guys.

Jade squeezes my leg and leans in. "What's wrong? Loosen up a little. You look so tense."

I pull my eyes away from Knight, who hasn't seemed to take his off of me since we sat down at our now joined tables. "I'm fine." I cover my head as one of the guys at the table stands up and starts tossing beers across the room to other tables, while drunkenly screaming. "These guys are just really fucking drunk and stupid. If one hits us with a beer, I'll kick them in the balls."

"You want to move? We can, but there aren't any other tables available. We're lucky we found this one."

Ducking around the crowded table, I begin looking around to see where we can possibly move to, when a beer flies right next to my head, almost hitting me.

Instinctively, my arm goes up to cover my head and anger floods through me. These dicks just really don't give a shit and I'm not about to spend the whole night dodging beers.

I stand up and grab Jade's arm, while keeping my eyes on the asshole with the beers. "We're moving. I don't care if we have to stand, but we're not staying here and getting knocked out by flying beers."

My heart about beats out of my chest, when Stone appears out of what seems like nowhere, and grabs the drunken guy by his shirt, slamming him into the table.

"Watch where the fuck you're throwing those beers, Asshole. Hit one of those girls and I'll fuck your shit up."

Knight stands up and rushes over to help his friend when he notices him in trouble, but stops when he notices Stone and Kash, as if he's seen them before and doesn't want any trouble.

Instead, he places his hand on Stone's shoulder and says something to him that has Stone releasing his grip on his asshole friend.

"He's cut off for the night, Bro. No worries," Knight says loud enough for the whole table to hear. "You hear that? Tanner is done so don't send anymore shit his way. Let's just enjoy the night."

Pulling his eyes away from Knight, Stone walks over and pulls out the chair next to me. "You alright?"

Still in shock that a fight didn't just break out, I nod my head, thankful that he's here to calm them down. "I am now," I say with a hint of a smile. "Thanks for that. I *was* about to drag Jade out of here."

Kash pulls up an empty chair next to Jade and takes a seat, instantly grabbing her attention away from any other guy at the table.

I'm a little surprised, because the way she's been looking at Knight, I expected her to go after *him*, but she's over there smiling as if he's the cutest thing she's ever seen.

Pulling my chair to face him, Stone pulls me closer until I'm between his legs. "I've dealt with these fuckers before, and I wouldn't have hesitated to fight every single one of those fuckers if you got hit with that beer."

I suck in a breath, as he reaches out and swipes his thumb over my bottom lip. "Stop making that sexy little sound when you breathe, before I bend you over in front of everyone and give you a reason to."

Holy shit . . .

I didn't even realize I was softly moaning, while looking him over in his fitted white t-shirt and dark jeans until now. Not to mention him standing up for me to a table full of fighters and their friends practically had me fighting for air.

This man is beyond sexy in everything he does and says and there's no denying it.

Damn him for being so fucking cute and irresistible.

"I bet you wish that I'd let you," I say next to his ear, while patting his chest.

Smirking, he grabs my wrist as I'm about to pull away,

placing my hand back on his flexed chest. "I do . . . and you would."

I smile. I can't help it. I love this side of Stone, even though I know it will probably get me where I've been trying *not* to be. "What makes you think that?"

"Because you've always wanted to have sex in a public place and what better way to do that than with a male stripper that will make you scream until your throats raw?"

"Oh shit!" Jade yells from beside me. "I heard that. Someone's got one dirty mouth."

Apparently, so did Knight, because he glares over at Stone, looking pissed that these male strippers have our attention and he doesn't.

A fighter is *hot*, but nothing is *hotter* than a man that can move his body in the dirty way that these *W.O.S* boys do.

Knight looks like he's about to say something, but gets distracted when a female throws her arms around his neck and begins whispering in his ear.

Relief washes over me, because having Stone get into a fight is the last thing I want right now, especially with some MMA fighters.

"Need another beer?" Stone questions.

I point at his empty hands. "Where's yours?"

"I'm not drinking tonight."

"Why not?"

He stands up and grabs my waist, helping me to my feet. "Someone has to keep an eye on you with all these rowdy assholes here eyeing you up."

Grabbing my hand, he pulls me through the crowd and over to the bar, holding onto me protectively.

Smiling, I watch as he orders two beers, I'm guessing one for Jade since Kash didn't look like he was drinking either.

As we're about to walk back over to the table, two girls stop Stone, acting all giddy and excited as if they've just spotted a celebrity or some shit.

"Come dance with us," one girl says.

"None of these other guys here tonight can dance. Please, Stone. Come play with us." The tall redhead smiles, but then gives me a dirty as hell look when she notices Stone holding my hand.

It pisses me off, yet makes me feel good that these other girls want him, and it's my hand that he's holding right now.

It has the feisty Sage wanting to come out and play. Bitch better back off.

"I'd watch that face because bitch does not look good on you, Honey."

Stone smiles as if he's impressed and then surprises me when he pulls me into him and runs his tongue across my lips, before biting the bottom one, causing my insides to jump with excitement. "Fuck me, Sage. You're sexy as fuck when you're feisty. Feel that?" He presses his hips into me, showing me that he's now hard. "Your mouth does this to me."

The girls give up and walk away, looking pissed that he didn't pay them any attention.

"Keep poking me with your *big* dick and I might just bite it." I smile against his ear. "Nice and hard. I don't think you want that."

I get ready to walk away with the beers, but Stone presses up behind me, wrapping his arm around my waist.

My pussy clenches as he bites my ear and possessively grips the button on my jeans as if he can rip it off any second and take me how he wants. "I'll take your mouth on my dick anyway you want. Don't think that a little pain will scare me. It will only make me fuck you harder."

Jade whistles, getting our attention as her and Kash stand up as if their ready to move somewhere else.

"Not tonight, Big guy," I manage to get out, even though my whole body is buzzing with need.

Wriggling out of his grip, I make my way over to Jade and hand her a beer, while following her over by the dartboards.

We start up a game and I try my best to not imagine Stone fucking me here in public and making me scream, but the way he keeps looking at me, makes it impossible to stop imagining.

It doesn't help any that those jeans he's wearing fit him so damn perfectly that any girl wouldn't be able to think straight after setting sight on his backside.

I swear my eyes have been glued to his firm ass every single time that he goes up to throw his darts.

I want to bite it.

"There's so much sexual tension between you and Stone that it's getting *my* dick hard," Kash whispers next to my ear, just as I'm about to throw my dart.

Laughing, I elbow him in the stomach, causing him to grunt and step back. "Stop trying to distract me just because I'm kicking your ass."

"Hey, I speak the truth." He wraps his arm around my neck and kisses my cheek. "Think Jade's into me? She keeps looking at my crotch and shit."

I look behind me to see Stone and Jade at the small table, talking, but her eyes keep lingering over to Kash's ass as if she can't control them.

"I'm going to take a wild guess and say yes." Smiling, I slap his chest and push him out of my space. "Now move the fuck out of my way so I can finish winning."

"Damn, Baby." Kash throws his arms up and backs up. "No wonder why Stone likes you so much. I might just take you home tonight if you'll let me. I'll take both you ladies on."

Stone continues talking to Jade, but slaps Kash upside the head, causing him to turn around in surprise.

"Watch your fucking mouth, Dumb ass."

Jade looks at Kash as if she likes what he just said. She winks and he pushes down on his boner, making it aware of what she does to him.

I throw my second dart and turn around to Stone standing right behind me. "I can't stop thinking about slamming you up against that wall, holding you above my head, and tasting you, Sage."

The way he draws his bottom lip into his mouth after he's done talking, has me almost panting, but I fight it.

Stay strong . . . don't cave in.

"Stop trying to distract me," I breathe, as he steps up behind me and presses his body to mine. "It's not going to work."

He grips my hips with both hands and softly kisses the back of my neck. "You sure about that?" His hands squeeze my hips and he slightly lifts me up to press his erection against my ass. "Take a shot then. Go ahead," he whispers.

Clearing my throat, I bump him with my ass to get him to release me. "Back up, Smart ass." Trying hard to focus, I throw my last dart, almost completely missing the board. "Shit."

Stone smiles in victory, before slapping my ass. "You ready to go home?" He nods his head at Kash and Jade all up close and personal with each other. "I think Kash is going to drive Jade's jeep to her house. I'll drive us."

Figuring that the game will take forever to finish, as long as it's been taking us to pay attention to our turns, I agree it's time to go.

After saying bye to Jade and Kash, Stone walks me to his jeep and opens the door for me.

He's quiet the whole way home as if he's thinking really hard about something, so I stay quiet too, not really sure what's going to happen when we get home.

I hope it's not some weird, awkward moment. We haven't really gotten any time alone since he danced for me the other night.

I'm not sure if I'll be able to tell him no after that . . .

STONE

THERE'S SOMETHING I WANT TO do to Sage as soon as I get her alone and I'm over here trying to decide if she'll kick my ass for even attempting it.

I figure the risk will be worth it. I'll take an ass whooping from her any day of the fucking week as long as it involves her hands on me.

Just the thought alone of her being rough with me makes me hard. So damn hard.

Hoping that she'll follow me, I walk around to the back of the house instead of the front, opening the gate to the pool.

I don't hesitate with yanking my shirt over my head, before dropping my jeans and kicking them to the side.

"What are you doing?" she asks, while watching my legs flex as I walk over to her.

"It's what *we're* doing."

Keeping my eyes on hers, I lower to the ground, grip the waist of her jeans and rip the button off, pulling until their unzipped.

Surprised, she grips my hair and pulls as I yank her jeans down her legs, before lifting her up enough to pull her feet out of them.

"Stone!" she yells. "Don't throw me in that pool or I'll kick your ass. I'll hurt you, I swear."

"Is that a promise?" I question with a smirk, while lifting her up to throw her over my shoulder.

"I mean it. Don't do it," she squeals. "It's cold."

Holding on to her tightly, I walk over to the water and jump in, not releasing my grip on her, until we hit the coolness of the water.

When we come up from under the water, Sage rushes at me, slapping my chest with her hand. "What. Did. I. Say," she questions, between each hard smack. "I'm going to . . . to . . . ."

"What was that?" I cup my ear and lean in closer, when she continues to mumble, coming up with nothing to say. "If you want me to make you come, all you have to do is say so. I'm more than happy to."

Pulling her over to the shallow end, I cup her pussy with my hand and lift her up with a growl, before sliding her panties aside and slipping one finger inside.

She grips at my shoulder and moans beside my ear as I slowly begin pumping in and out, while backing her up against the wall of the pool.

"Damn you and your perfect fingers," she breathes.

"I don't have to use my fingers," I respond, while shoving a second one inside. "I can do much better."

"That wasn't an invitation," she growls out. "I think we should . . ." she throws her head back with a moan when I swirl my finger over her swollen clit.

"Just give your body what it wants, Sage."

Lifting her up, I position Sage so her legs are straddling my shoulders and her soaking wet panties are pressed against my face.

Squeezing my head with her thighs, she screams and pulls my hair with force. "You're pushing it, Stone. So fucking close to the edge. Put me down before I kick your ass."

"Go ahead . . . hurt me," I warn. "I'll make you scream with my tongue so fucking loud that the neighbors will get off on it."

Pushing me, she squeezes my face tighter. "You won't . . ."

"Oh I will, Beautiful girl." I gently bite her pussy, causing her to yank on my hair. "You like my mouth between your legs. Admit it."

Pushing her body closer so I can tease her, I suck her clit into my mouth through her thin, wet panties, sucking so hard that she cries out with a mixture of pain and pleasure.

"Stone," she moans my name this time in desperation. "Get my fucking panties out of the way, dammit."

Licking her through the fabric, I suck her clit into my mouth once more, before releasing it. "Admit it then."

"I miss it," she breathes. "And I'm going to kill you later for making me admit it, but for now . . ."

She pushes my head between her legs and leans back with another moan as I rub my face in her pussy and growl against it.

I set her down on edge of the pool so I can remove her wet panties.

Then I sink into the water in front of her, before coming back up, spreading her legs apart, and running my stiff tongue along her aching pussy.

"Take your shirt off," I growl out. "I want to see your nipples harden when I taste you. They always got so fucking hard for me."

Without hesitation, she removes her shirt, before undoing

her bra and tossing it behind her. "This is as far as it goes," she attempts to say with force. "No sex. We just . . . just no sex."

I may not be having sex with her tonight, but her letting me pleasure her with my tongue is the only sign that I need, to know that she still aches for me just as much as I do her.

Tonight . . . tonight she's going to remember what it's like to have my tongue taste her so damn good that she's going to beg me to please her in every way possible by the end of the week.

Gripping her legs, I moan as I look over her naked body, remembering what it was like to have her above me, riding me.

"Fuck . . . I've missed pleasuring this beautiful body." Reaching up with one hand, I cup her left breast and bury my face between her legs.

My tongue works slowly at first to spread the moisture up her folds, being gentle and teasing her, making her want more. My rhythm is precise and in control, knowing the exact spot to work her up. I'm slowly building her up, knowing she'll want more at the end.

I catch her moaning as I slide my tongue down further and shove it into her pussy as deep as it will go. I'm fucking her with my tongue, working her up to want me back inside of her.

She rips and pulls at my hair, pushing my face further between her legs as if she wants to suffocate me with her beautiful vagina.

I'd die a happy man and ask one of the boys to inscribe it on my fucking headstone.

Pulling my tongue out, I gently suck her clit into my mouth, sucking on it, while shoving a finger inside her and pumping in and out.

This used to drive her crazy and I'm hoping it still does.

From the way that she digs into my back and squeezes my head, I'm going to take that as a *fucking hell yes.*

"Oh fuck," she moans. "Shit, Stone. Keep going." Her hands rip at my hair now. "I'm so close. I'm close . . . fuck!"

Her legs shake above my shoulders as her pussy clenches around my finger so damn hard that it's almost as if she's been deprived of orgasms since we stopped messing around months ago.

A part of me is relieved, yet the other part of me wants her to feel good all of the time.

Fuck, I feel guilty for not pushing this sooner and making her cave into me pleasuring her.

I kiss the inside of her thighs, before releasing her as she slides back into the water, breathing heavily.

She doesn't look at me or speak for what seems like five fucking minutes, which has my heart completely pounding out of my chest in anticipation.

"I almost forgot how good your mouth felt," she says, still out of breath. "Your mouth has always been my weakness."

She dives into the water, swimming over to the deep end.

Smiling, I watch her as she comes up for air.

"I couldn't let you forget. I won't."

"Then are you sure we should still be roommates?" she asks with a slight grin. "This could get complicated. Do we want that?"

Biting my bottom lip, I swim over to her and wrap her legs around my waist. "The more complicated . . . the better satisfying that it is in the end when we both give in."

I cup her face.

"What are you doing?" she asks, sounding slightly panicked.

"Giving you a good night kiss."

Before she can say anything, I press my lips against hers, claiming them like in the past, before slowly caressing my tongue with hers as her lips part. It's soft, slow and hot as fuck.

Our tongues instantly work together as if we've never stopped kissing to begin with. It's so fucking natural that my dick twitches, at the fact that we were made to be doing this. Stone and fucking Sage . . . together.

Now, I'm determined more than ever to get her into my arms for good.

Sucking her bottom lip into my mouth, I release it and pull away with a small growl. "I also couldn't let you forget my mouth on yours."

Licking her lips, she turns her face away from me. "Goodnight, Stone."

I release her from my arms, watching as she swims over to the edge of the pool and climbs out, completely naked.

Holy fuck . . . she's beautiful.

"Goodnight," I whisper, mostly to myself as she disappears into the house, leaving me hard as fuck in this pool.

As much as I'd love to sink into her and remind her how good I feel inside of her, I know I can't move that fast if I want to make her fall for me.

I need to remind her of the small things first.

My dick will have to wait . . .

chapter TEN

Sage

I HAVEN'T SEEN STONE SINCE last night in the pool, when he shamelessly made me come from that damn magic mouth of his. By the time I got off work this evening, he was already at W.O.S and he won't be home until late tonight.

Why does this disappoint me?

I've been thinking about him all day and smiling to my damn self like an idiot. I almost feel like a teenaged girl, finding out that her crush likes her back.

So damn weird . . .

Lying in bed, eating chicken and rice, in my underwear and a tank top, I struggle between wanting to go to the club and telling myself that I'd be stupid to go.

If I go see him, it'll give him the impression that I want him again and that it's okay for him to do whatever he pleases with me.

As much as I want a physical relationship with him, I'm not sure I can handle that without blurring the lines, falling for him and wanting more.

I came so close in the past to losing myself to him. Too close. And I know if I let myself care for him and then lose him, I'll be devastated.

I'm not heartless. I care for Stone. I care for him very much, but after being crushed over and over again by every person that I ever cared for or thought should've cared for me, I'm not sure I'm strong enough.

I want to be. So damn bad.

"You're staying right here in this bed," I mumble to myself, while stuffing my face with rice. "You've been strong for over seven months now. Don't. Cave. In."

Picking up the remote, I flip through the hundreds of channels, but can't seem to concentrate on anything that's on. Not one damn thing.

All I can think about is Stone and the fact that he's got hundreds of women clawing at his half-naked ass right now, wanting him to pleasure them with his magic fucking *everything.*

Shoving the now empty container aside, I reach for my phone when it vibrates next to me. I get excited for a quick second, thinking it might be Stone, but it's not.

It's a message from Jade.

Jade: Whatcha doing? You better be awake.

Me: Laying around and watching TV. I'm still awake, unfortunately.

Jade: Get your ass up and dressed. Kash is dancing tonight and he invited me to watch him.

Me: Yeah . . . can't you go alone? I have to be up early tomorrow.

Jade: Um . . . no. I need you there. PLEASE!

Me: Put your big girl panties on, Jade. I'm tired.

Jade: I can't. I need help pulling them up. PLEASE! PLEASE! PLEASE!

Me: I hate you sometimes . . .

Jade: Is that a yes, gorgeous?

Me: It's a maybe . . .

My phone doesn't go off for the next five minutes, so I just lay here and struggle with my damn self.

I almost think that Jade has given up on me, until it vibrates again, causing me to sit up and exhale.

Picking it up, I get ready to tell her I'll go, but the name that flashes across the screen has my stomach doing backflips and my heart beating out of my chest. Yeah . . . it's like *that* with him.

Stone: I can still taste you on my tongue . . . so distracting. Do you know how hard it is to not pop a boner every few minutes?

His text has me laughing out loud and trying hard to stop myself from smiling, but I can't. I can only picture his face right now and how he probably has that one brow lifted as he types with that cocky ass grin of his.

Me: You could try mouthwash. Have you ever heard of it? There's a bottle in our bathroom. That might control your boner. ;)

Stone: And wash the delectable taste of your throbbing pussy out of my mouth . . . how else am I going to get through the night without you?

Me: Who says you have to?

Seriously, Sage!

I mentally slap myself for allowing myself to flirt back and work him up even more than he already is, knowing where that might lead later. Last night was already pushing the friend-zone limit.

Stone: Is that an invitation? Cause' I accept with my mouth wide open.

Me: You really are something else . . .

Stone: I've been told that's a good thing. By you . . .

He's not wrong there. His playful personality and non-filtered mouth is what made me want him in the first place. It made me feel happy and . . . alive.

Stone: Gotta go. See you later, roomie ;)

I jump when my bedroom door flies open to Jade coming at me with a look of disappointment.

"Why the hell isn't your ass dressed? Kash goes on in less than twenty minutes. Hurry! Get up!"

"Seriously?" Standing up, I brush past her and slip on a pair of jeans. "What made you so sure I'd even go? I never said yes."

"Because . . ." she smiles as I change into a cute, red blouse and quickly throw my hair up. "You didn't say no."

"I'll go." I hold up a hand, while slipping on a pair of black heels. "But only for a couple of hours. I'm gone before midnight so don't even bother with trying to get me to stay 'til close."

"Deal." Her smile broadens. "You do realize that Stone will

be dancing right after Kash, right? So that's within the next hour."

"I do." I lift a brow and smile to myself. "So, I'll be gone *after* he dances. If I'm going, might as well make it worth it for me too, Babe."

"I won't argue there." She looks down at her phone, before grabbing my arm and pulling me through the house with her. "Ten minutes now. I don't want to miss even a second."

Surprisingly, Jade has never seen Kash dance. In fact, I think she's only been to *W.O.S* a few times and that was before Kash started.

It should be interesting to see her reaction when she sees just how dirty Kash can be on the stage.

He's dirty . . . but not as dirty as Stone or Styx.

***

IT'S INSANELY CROWDED HERE TONIGHT, but Lane worked his magic to find us tables right in the front row.

I have a feeling that Cale had something to do with that. He smiled at us from across the room as we were walking in, then right after that, Lane was talking into his earpiece.

God, I love that man. He's the cutest thing ever and does what he can to make sure everyone's happy. Not to mention that he's an amazing dad and family man.

Him taking over *W.O.S* has been the best thing for this place. The changes he made by adding private rooms has pretty much doubled business, making it possible for the boys to bring in a shitload of money.

Not that the boys weren't already.

"Here he comes." Jade slaps my arm, getting all giddy, when Kash appears on the darkened stage. "Is that a uniform? Please tell me he's in uniform. Oh please," she begs.

The music starts and the spotlight lands on Kash, standing

there in a police uniform.

Oh shit . . . not tonight.

The last thing I can handle right now is Stone in uniform. I completely forgot that it was theme night, which means all of the boys will be dressed up.

Each week one of the boys chooses which theme they want and all of the boys go along with it.

I've never seen Stone in a police uniform, because I've always made it a point to stay away when I knew he'd be looking that damn sexy.

Police officers are my weakness.

I miss the first five minutes of Kash's dance, lost in my head, worrying about Stone coming out next.

"This man is the sexiest thing I've ever seen, Sage. *The* sexiest."

When I look up, Kash is already half-naked and dry humping the stage.

Jade stands up and walks up to the stage, when Kash motions for her come up.

I find myself laughing at her facial expression, as he pulls her onto the stage and forces her onto her knees and into a pair of cuffs.

Grabbing her cuffs from behind her, he begins thrusting his hips insanely fast, causing her body to bounce forward with each hard thrust.

The girls go crazy, standing up and tossing money toward the stage, loving how rough and dirty he is.

Knowing that it's about time for Stone to take the stage, I begin looking around me, in search of him standing in the shadows.

He does this *before* every show, standing back with his black beanie, trying not to stand out.

"Holy shit!" Jade breathes heavily, from beside me. "That was insane. That boy can move his body."

Pulling my eyes away from the back of the room, I turn to face Jade. She's sweaty and out of breath, fanning herself off.

"These boys are the best of the best."

Disappointment washes through me that I didn't get a glimpse of Stone before his show.

I always enjoyed seeking him out in the shadows and watching him look so damn mysterious in the darkened room.

"Here comes your sexy roommate," Jade says excitedly. "You ready, Babe?"

My heart speeds up as the music starts. "I fucking hope so."

Holy fuck . . . help me now . . .

chapter ELEVEN

Sage

THE UNIFORM THAT STONE IS wearing is form fitting, clinging to his hard, muscled chest and showing off his tatted arms.

I've never seen someone look so damn sexy in uniform until now and I have to admit that my heart is practically palpitating out of chest, as my eyes search over his entire body.

Does this man not know just how hard he'll have the ladies clenching by the end of his performance? Me included.

It's not until the spotlight grows bigger, revealing more of the stage, that I notice there's a girl with blue hair and tattoos handcuffed to a chair.

His performances seem to be so damn mysterious now, compared to seven months ago and completely fucking hotter.

I don't even want to think about how that sexy chick got chosen to be a part of his performance, but I'm hoping it wasn't by him.

"Oh wow . . ." Jade takes a huge gulp of her drink, while eyeing the stage. "This could get hot. Stone looks good in uniform.

Really good."

Swallowing, I blindly reach beside me for my drink, not wanting to miss a thing. I have a feeling that I'm going to need a few of these after he's done.

"The man's got a body of a God, Jade. You try living with all of *that* and be able to keep any kind of self-control. It's a bitch and that uniform is doing zilch to help the situation any."

"So, then give in. I would. Especially after all of *that* looks like *that* in uniform."

Letting Jade's words sink in, I keep my eyes glued to Stone's every move as he slowly circles around the girl, before standing in front of the chair and grabbing the back of the girl's hair, thrusting to the rhythm.

Oh. God.

The girl instantly bites her lip and watches his dick flopping through his pants, probably wishing she could take him in her mouth right now.

Hell . . . even I am, from the way his body's moving so damn hot and in perfect rhythm to the sexy song.

His dick doesn't even have to be close my face to want it just as badly as she probably does at this very moment. It doesn't help that I've had a taste and it's the best of the best. There's no denying how damn delicious every inch of that man's body truly is.

Gripping the top of his shirt, Stone slowly rips it open, while rolling his body above her in the chair, before tossing the fabric aside.

Her eyes widen and she begins screaming with excitement as he climbs up on the chair, making it easier to thrust in her face.

Afterwards, he lowers himself down to straddle her lap, reaching behind her to undo her cuffs.

The woman's hands instantly find Stone's body, exploring as

he grinds in her lap. Grabbing her hands to stop them from going for his dick, he stands up and turns around, before taking a seat on her lap again, but facing the crowd this time.

Taking control of the woman's hands again, Stone rubs them up the inside of his thick thighs before, making her explore his abs and then his chest as he rolls his body, making the women scream out.

Keeping in his intense roll as an officer, he pushes her hands away and stands up, turning around to face her again, before lowering to her lap and thrusting with force as if she's been a bad girl.

When he goes to get out of the cute girl's lap, she grips his face, pressing her lips against his with force.

My heart explodes with jealousy and anger, but I watch intently, as Stone pulls away from the kiss and backs away from her.

He looks a little thrown off, but falls back into beat with the song, smoothly picking the girl up out of the chair, doing a few small thrusts, before carrying her off stage and setting her down into an empty seat.

That's when his eyes finally seek me out for the first time. He looks excited to see me here, yet guilty or ashamed, possibly, at me seeing another woman kiss him.

I just give him a small smile and lift my drink to him, showing him that I'm not going anywhere. Someone would have to drag me out of here at this point, because I'm not taking my eyes off this sexy man until he's done.

He grins back and continues with the show, keeping his eyes on me as often as he can, while stripping down until he's down to absolutely nothing, only holding his pants over his junk.

The song is almost over now, since Stone had to waste time to walk off stage and dispose of his overzealous fan, so he does a few more quick thrusts of his hips, before dropping his pants on the stage and using both of his hands to cover up.

Keeping both of his hands covering his package, he exits the stage and walks straight for mine and Jade's table.

Whistles and screams are deafening me at this point, but I can't help but to smile as Stone's eyes look me over, before stopping to meet mine.

Leaning into my ear, he whispers, "I'm trying really fucking hard to cover how hard you have me right now. Now would be a good time to have a third hand." He lets out a deep laugh, vibrating my ear and turning me on even more. "Wait for me."

Nodding my head, I bite my straw and watch as he walks away, women all jumping to slap his naked, tight ass as he walks away.

STONE'S SHOW ENDED TWENTY MINUTES ago and I've been waiting impatiently for him to come back out.

I can't deny the fact that I want him sexually so bad right now, that it physically hurts. My body is screaming for him to touch me and pleasure me to the point that I almost feel desperate to have him inside of me.

Seeing that Jade is preoccupied at the bar, talking with Sara, I make my way to the back area where the boys' locker room area is.

Kane is standing outside, guarding the door, but smiles when he sees me approaching.

"What's up, Babe?" He takes a second to turn back to the girl that's practically hanging on his nuts and kissing all over his neck. "Take it easy, Sugar."

"No need to stop on my account, you sexy giant." I lift a brow and flash the girl a tight smile when she looks me over, trying to size me up. "Let me in to see Stone and you can get your dick wet all you want."

Kane looks around, seeing that no one else seems to be coming back here, other than me.

"Only because it's you." He smiles big. "And because I'm afraid you'll kick my ass and I'll like it too much."

"Oh you definitely would like it, Kane. I know you." I wink and slap his chest. "Be sure not to break the poor girl in half. I've heard you fuck before." I turn to her. "I'd be scared myself."

This only seems to get the girl more excited and it somewhat makes me happy that I'm not the only one completely sexually frustrated at this second.

Plus, I need to keep him satisfied, reminding him that it was definitely worth his time to break the rules and let me in the boys' room.

Taking a deep breath, I push the door open and step inside to the steam filled room. The only thing I hear are the showers.

More than one.

The problem with this, is that you can't see shit through the thick glass doors.

I stop in front of the first one, not thinking twice, before pushing the glass door open and looking for Stone.

My face heats up when I'm greeted with the sight of Kash, naked, with soap and water running down the front of his insanely sexy body.

His eyes open and widen when they land on me watching him, following my eyes down to his partially hard dick.

"Shit! Sorry," I mouth to him. "Wrong door."

He just gives me a cocky ass smile, knowing damn well that he has nothing to be ashamed of.

Quickly closing Kash's door, I take in a deep breath, before reaching for the second door and pushing it open.

Stone is facing the shower wall, letting the water fall down his perfectly, tattooed, flawless body, while running his hands over his face.

Wanting nothing more than to touch every inch of him, I step into the shower and close the door behind me, pulling my blouse over my head and tossing it to the ground.

Stone stiffens up for a second, before he slowly turns around and smirks when he sees me standing here in only my bra and jeans, looking over his body.

Swallowing, I let my eyes trail down to his very hard, pierced dick and I completely lose it.

Throwing my arms around his neck, I slam my lips against his, as he grips my thighs, picking me up to wrap my legs around his waist.

He kisses me hard and hungry, before sucking my lip into his mouth and pulling away. "Fuck me, Sage. You're in my damn shower. I hope you know this means I'm stripping you down and fucking you."

Nodding my head, I dig into my pocket and pull out the condom, that I stole from Jade's purse when she was talking to Sara.

Growling out, Stone gently sets me down to my feet and bends down, yanking my jeans and thong down my legs.

He gets ready to lick my pussy, but I grip his head, pushing it back. "Not this time," I breathe, heavily. "I can't. I need you inside me right now, Stone and for you to promise me one thing?"

Standing back up, he brushes my hair behind my ear and kisses under my ear. "What's that?"

Biting my bottom lip, I watch as Stone rolls the condom over his enormous, pierced dick. "Don't ever wear that damn uniform again. That's not fair play."

Smirking, he lifts me up and slams me against the wall that's connected to Kash's shower. "Fuck yeah it is." He bites my lip and pulls away. "Especially if gets you this worked up."

Holding me up with one arm around my waist, he grips my neck with his free hand and slams into me so hard that I scream out with a mixture of pain and pleasure.

"Fuck me," he growls against my ear, while slowly pulling out of me, before pushing back inside and freezing. "It's been so damn long. You okay?"

Gripping onto his strong shoulders, I nod my head and moan as the pain goes away and all I'm left with is the feel of him slowly sliding in and out of me, filling me to capacity.

"It's okay," I breathe. "You can go now."

"Are you sure?" he questions. "I'm not holding back. I've waited too long to be inside you again, Sage. I'm going to fuck you as if it'll be my last. I didn't last time and I should've. Every. Fucking. Time."

Gripping him tighter, I pull his face to mine and kiss him hard and deep, just needing him to shut up and take me like he did the very first time.

I didn't walk for two days without wanting to cry from the pain between my legs.

Moaning into my mouth, he grips my neck harder and thrusts into me over and over again as if he's letting out all of his sexual frustration from the last seven months.

It's so hard and deep that it hurts, but I don't want it to stop.

Everything about Stone is pure alpha male and having him fuck me and take me as hard and deep as he wants, turns me on more than anyone I've ever been with.

Holding onto him for dear life, I bite his mouth so hard, when he thrusts into me, that I draw blood.

This causes him to growl into my mouth and slam into me even harder, causing my head to bang into the wall behind me.

The roughness of being with Stone is worth every bump and bruise I get in the process. When this man fucks, he owns my pussy as if telling me that no other dick will feel as good as his does inside of me.

The fact that Kash is in the next shower, listening to us, must turn us both on more, making us both get louder and louder with each time he pushes inside of me.

"Stone!" I scream. "Fuck. Me . . ." I breathe. "Don't stop."

He slams into me and stops. "Not until your pussy is clamping down on my cock," he breathes out in response.

"Oh shit . . ." Comes from Kash's shower, making us both smile against each other's lips, before he pushes into me one last time, pushing me over the edge as my pussy clenches his dick so hard, that I feel his hot cum filling the condom inside of me.

Holding me up, he walks me to the middle of the shower and kisses me as the water runs over the both of us, cooling us off now that the hot water has run out.

He waits until I pull away from the kiss, before pulling out of me and setting me down.

Turning the other way, he pulls the condom off with a small moan and tosses it down, while leaning his face back into the water.

I can't help the tingles that spread throughout my body as I watch him, standing there, breathing heavily in all his naked glory, throbbing dick and all.

There's something so sexy just knowing that his heavy breathing is due to him just being inside of me.

"Shit, that was hot, Sage." He turns to look at me with a small smirk. "I might just wear my uniform around the house every fucking night if it leads you to joining me in the shower."

I can't help but to laugh at the cute face he makes as he looks me over. "I'll burn it if I have to," I tease. "Don't test me."

Smiling as if he doesn't believe me, he turns the water off and walks out of the shower, before returning a few seconds later with a towel and wrapping it around me.

"Kash might've just gotten off to you screaming while I fucked you, but that asshole doesn't get to see or feel what it's like to have you naked and horny. I'll find you something to wear."

"Holy shit . . ." Smiling to myself, I work on drying myself off, while Stone is off finding me some clothes.

I'm pretty surprised that I actually just went through with showing up in his shower, ready to have sex, but am so happy that I did.

I've never felt so much excitement and adrenaline course through me in my entire life.

Just knowing that hundreds of people are outside that door, and that Kash was right next to us, jerking off to us fucking, has me wanting to do all sorts of crazy things with Stone.

I'm not so sure this is a feeling I'm ready to give up now. In fact . . . I want him sexually more now than ever.

STONE

IT'S MY DAY OFF, YET I'VE been stuck spending my day with Kash's horny ass, that can't seem to stop talking about mine and Sage's shower sex from two fucking days ago.

I swear if I see his dick get hard one more time, when he mentions the fact that Sage walked in on him in the shower and checked out his shit; I'm going to throat punch his bitch ass.

"You should've saw the way her eyes grew when they landed on my love muscle, Bro." He throws his last dart at the board, before walking up to retrieve them. "If I remember correctly, there may have even been a little lip biting action on her part."

"Fuck you, Dumb ass." I shoulder bump him on the way to the yellow line. "Her eyes grew bigger so she could find your little dangler."

Not fazed by my insult, he winks at the waitress and checks out her ass as she walks by.

"You mean the beast. Nope, she definitely got a clear view and he turned into Mr. Happy."

Choosing to ignore his ass, before I turn Mr. Happy into Mr. Fucking Sad, I throw my darts, before looking down at the time on my phone.

"I'm out of here, Dick."

Kash stands up and tosses a ten on top of my twenty. "Same here, man. I've got some shit to handle. I heard Sage gets off in twenty."

I walk past him and slap him hard, upside the head. "Later, Fucker."

He's right, Sage does get off in twenty and I'm hoping to get her to hang out with me.

After we left *W.O.S* the other night, she went to her room to sleep, while I spent most of the night, chillin' on the balcony.

Sage worked all day yesterday and I worked all night, so by the time I got home, she was already in her bed.

She left the door cracked open and I about lost my shit when I walked by and saw what she was sleeping in.

A sheer, white shirt with no bra and a pale pink thong, displaying her perfect round ass.

The way her pierced nipples pressed against the fabric, caused my dick to instantly harden in my jeans.

I thought about waking her up, by taking her nipple into my mouth and nibbling it, but decided that might lead to me being kicked in the balls or my dick being ripped off.

That woman is feisty when it comes to her sleep. I woke her up once when I was drunk and it was not a good time for me. Trust me.

I had a shoeprint on my forehead for two days from than damn Converse, but I guess I had it coming with my teasing.

We both laughed about it for weeks. In fact, the whole damn crew did.

It didn't bother me though, because seeing her laugh always

made me so fucking happy. I'd let her laugh at my expense every damn day just to keep that woman laughing.

When I arrive at the house with pizza and wings, Sage is just walking up to the porch.

She looks exhausted, as if she didn't sleep much last night, but flashes me a thankful smile, when I hold up the food and wink.

"You read my mind, Big guy." She unlocks the door and pushes it open, making room for me to carry the food through.

"I'd like to read your whole body with my tongue, but I thought I'd start with pizza first and work my way there."

She laughs and bumps me out of the way with her hip, to get to the pizza. "I really don't know what to do with you some days. Do you know that?"

"So does that mean buying you pizza won't get me in your pants tonight?" I hold up the wings and cock a brow. "What if I toss in a few wings?"

She laughs harder, almost spitting her pizza all over the counter. It takes her a few seconds to catch her breath. "You're really laying the charm on extra hard tonight, Prince Charming. You make it so hard to resist, but . . . I'm not that easy."

I shrug and grab a slice of pizza. "Yeah well . . . I am." I wink. "Just for future reference."

"Aren't all of you dirty boys."

"Abso-fuckin-lutely. Thirsty?" I ask, while walking to the fridge.

Biting into her pizza, she nods her head and mumbles, "Yes," around it.

Knowing that she'll probably want some white wine, I pour her a glass, before grabbing myself a beer and walking outside to the second story balcony.

I smile to myself, when I hear her following behind me,

carrying the whole pizza box, and moaning whenever she takes a bite of the slice in her hand.

"You really should be careful about moaning around me. You know I see that as a challenge if it's not from my doing."

She ignores me and reaches for a second slice of pizza, while sitting on the ledge of the balcony. "I think you made me moan loud enough the other night to make up for a thousand damn moans."

My smile broadens as her eyes meet mine, before slowly trailing down my body and landing on my half-hard dick. The seductive way she licks the pizza from her lips, makes me believe that she wishes it were my cum.

Well fuck . . . I do too.

Clearing her throat, she quickly pulls her eyes away and finishes up her slice of pizza.

I take a swig of my beer and hand her glass of wine to her, before taking a seat beside her and watching her take a sip. "How was work?"

She shrugs. "It was okay, I guess. Onyx almost ripped some girl's tit off, but you know how that goes . . ."

I laugh, trying to picture that in my head. "Yeah, well she definitely doesn't take any shit from anyone. Her and Hemy were meant to fucking be."

"More than any two people I know," she replies, her eyes softening as they land on mine again. "I'm pretty tired."

"Then relax and drink your wine," I respond. "It's beautiful out tonight."

She places her lips to her glass and smiles. "It is . . . the problem is . . ."

"What's that?" I question, while licking my bottom lip. "You can't stop thinking about me bending you over this balcony and filling you with my cock?"

She crosses her legs and takes another sip of her wine, but a longer one this time. Actually, more like she downs the whole fucking glass.

"The setting is too romantic," she finally answers.

"Doesn't have to be." I reply, while bending down in front of her and spreading her thighs. "I can make it dirty. Filthy and hard is my specialty."

Pushing her dress up, I bite the inside of her thigh, causing her to scream and pull my hair with force.

"Dammit, Stone. You know I love it when you bite me." She pushes my head back. "It's too soon though."

"You sure about that?" She loosens her grip on my head, just enough for me to swipe my tongue over her pussy lips that are practically hanging out of her thong.

Her legs shake as she pushes my head back again and attempts to close her legs. "Yes," she moans. "It's been less than forty-eight hours, Stone."

Standing up, I rub my hand over the erection in my jeans and take a huge swig of my beer. "Fuck . . . that's going to hurt later."

Sage sucks her bottom lip into her mouth, while watching my hand press down on my insanely hard cock.

"Let me watch you," she breathes. "It's too soon to be physical with each other, but doesn't mean I don't want to see you cum."

I set my beer down and look at her. "You want me to jerk off for you?"

She sits up straight and grips the ledge. "Yeah." She swallows. "Right here in the open."

Looking around me is a reminder of just how close the houses in this neighborhood are. Getting sexual in the pool is a little different since there's a huge fence for privacy, but up here . . . Up here you can see *everything*.

"You want me to whip my huge, throbbing cock out and stroke it right here for you?" Biting my bottom lip, I slowly undo my pants and step closer to her. "For anyone in the neighborhood to see? Cause' they can very well be watching us right now."

She nods her head and finishes off her wine, before setting it aside with a playful smirk. "I'm so fucking horny right now, Stone. *You* get me so damn horny and wet. I'm trying to keep some kind of self-control, before I lose it all, but I can't deny that I want to see you give me a show right here."

The idea of stroking my cock for her and possibly for the neighbors to see, is really fucking turning me on for some reason. My dick is throbbing now.

"Fuck . . . it's so damn hard." I growl, while unzipping my jeans and pulling them down to my thighs. "I love it when you talk to me so damn hot like this."

"Good," she breathes, while keeping her eyes on my hands to see where they're going next. "Take it out and hold it in your hand. Please," she says on a small breath.

Obeying her orders, I lower my briefs, pulling my cock out and holding it in my hand. "Fuck me . . . this has me so horny right now."

"Me too." She grips her thigh, running her fingers over it. "Now stroke it for me."

Grabbing my length with my other hand, I work both hands over my cock, moaning at the sensation and the fact that Sage along with who knows who else, is watching me pleasure myself right now.

I start out slow, closing my eyes and picturing Sage's warm mouth wrapped around my dick.

The thought gets me so excited, that I growl out in pleasure, feeling the pressure already starting to build.

A small moan leaves Sage's mouth when I stroke it harder and faster, while biting down onto my lower lip.

Opening my eyes, I watch as Sage dips her fingers and out of her pussy, while watching me stroke myself.

"Keep going, Stone," she moans. "Stroke it faster." She sounds desperate as her fingers speed up and she begins shaking as her orgasm rolls through her.

Hearing the wetness as she pumps in and out a few more times, is all it takes for me to lose my shit myself.

Stepping up beside her, I give her a clear view and aim my cock over the balcony, moaning out as my cum comes out in spurts, the pressure building and falling, until it finally stops completely and I can catch my breath.

I have no idea if anyone other than Sage just watched me shoot my shit over the balcony, but I can say that I just had one of the most intense orgasms of my life. At least one given from my own damn hand.

"Oh shit . . ." I breathe, while bending over and gripping the balcony. "That shot far," I tease. "Maybe even in the neighbor's yard."

Smiling, while trying to catch her breath, Sage adjusts her skirt and stands up. "You always know how to lighten the mood."

I smile as she looks me over. "Wondering how many people just watched me bust my nut for you?"

"Maybe," she grins. "Lucky them."

"I won't argue that," I respond with a cocked brow.

Clearing her throat, she reaches for her empty wine glass and walks for the door. "I think I'll have those wings now." She smiles. "Then I'm thinking we can just sit out here and talk for a bit."

I reach for my jeans and fix them, while watching her disappear inside. The excitement of what I've just done still has adrenaline pumping through my veins, making me feel wide awake now.

I'm prepared to talk her up all damn night, reminding her of how much fun we used to have just hanging out.

After what she just asked of me . . . I'm not letting her ass sleep for a while.

chapter
THIRTEEN

Sage

AFTER SPENDING HOURS TALKING TO Stone last night on the balcony, I fell asleep hard, sleeping like a baby, until my alarm woke me up for work this morning.

I almost forgot how fun it was to just hang out with Stone and laugh and forget about everything else. He's always had a way of relaxing me and making me feel good, as if nothing bad is in the world.

By the time I made it to my bedroom late last night, my face hurt from smiling so much and I'm pretty sure that I fell asleep, still wearing a smile because of him.

I have to admit that I've been a bit out of it this morning and even got caught napping in the breakroom earlier today by Onyx.

Apparently, I've forgotten what it's like to stay up late and get my ass up so early. It's been months since I've stayed up past two.

I've just finished cleaning off my station, when I walk up to the counter to see Onyx take a card from a thick, pretty brunette with cowgirl boots.

Out of curiosity, my eyes wander down to the card in Onyx's hand and my heart drops, when I see Stone's name written across it.

The only thing I can seem to concentrate on now is her mouth and what's going to come out of it.

"Follow me," Onyx says with a friendly smile, before leading her over to her station, which luckily, happens to be right next to mine.

Or maybe in my case . . . unluckily. I'm about to find out.

"Sage," Aspen calls from the front. "Your three o'clock is here. You ready?"

"Shit," I mutter under my breath. "Send them back."

Talk about bad timing.

I smile to my client and make small talk, while getting her ready, but my mind is stuck on Onyx and her client, wanting to hear what they're talking about.

I keep leaning their way, feeling like a crazy stalker at this point. I have no idea why I even care so much. *Just friends . . .* I remind myself. *Roommates. Friends . . . with benefits?*

My client talking, while I'm off in my own little stalking world, trying to listen to a totally different conversation, is making it pretty much impossible to concentrate.

I'm doing everything I can to not mess up her beautiful, thick hair, but I'm not feeling very confident at the moment.

Get it together . . .

Shaking my head, I take a deep breath and give up on trying to listen to what's being said at Onyx's station. So far, Stone's name hasn't left Ms. Country girl's red, pouty lips.

I'll just have to ask Onyx about their conversation as soon as we're both done, even though it's really none of my business, but as hard as I'm trying to not care . . . I do.

Half way through cutting my client's hair, she finally shuts up and suddenly the whole salon seems extremely quiet, as if both Aspen and Onyx can feel my stress.

Out of nowhere Onyx asks the one thing that I've been stressing over since her client walked through the door. She definitely must be able to tell just how tense I'm looking and feeling right now.

"So how was your experience at *W.O.S?* Did the boys treat you good? I hope so, or I'll have to kick their asses and remind them how it's done."

My body stiffens, waiting on her response and my heart is hammering in my chest. It's crazy how I feel right now.

She laughs softly. "They did," she says in a sweet southern accent. "I'm here visiting an old friend and I've never been to a male strip club before so she begged me to go. I'm glad I caved in. The boys were fantastic. Especially that Stone guy. He was so darn cute."

Aspen and Onyx stay quiet for a moment, probably worried about how I might react if she says they hooked up.

Clearing her throat, Onyx asks, "Did you get a private dance from Stone? Or . . ."

She laughs, embarrassed. "Oh no . . . no. Nothing like that. I'd be too chicken to be alone with one of those cuties. They look like movie stars. I was sweating like a pig." She smiles. "He just happened to hand me a card after his show and flashed me the most beautiful smile I've ever seen. My friend about had to pick me up off the floor."

I find myself smiling when she talks about Stone's smile and how beautiful it is. That's one of the first things I noticed about him when I first laid eyes on him and it still makes me weak.

His smile just glows and radiates this confidence, but also

has this sexy sweetness to it that makes you want to melt into a puddle at his feet.

The man is extremely hard to resist and after the show he gave me last night . . . Oh. My. God. I want him even more. I just have to keep reminding myself in which way so the lines don't get blurred even more than already have.

After I get off work and get home, I do a little cleaning, before checking my phone for any notifications. My heart practically jumps out of my chest with excitement when I see a missed text from Stone.

I've been contemplating sending him a message all day, but kind of wanted him to message me first.

It's kind of his thing.

> *Stone: My hand hurts from last night. I had to work extra hard to put on a good show. Want to make it up to me? ;)*

> *Me: Ha! Ha! What's the problem? Not used to jerking off on public balconies?*

> *Stone: No . . . but I kind of enjoyed it. From the sounds of your wet pussy, I'm taking it you did too. *winks**

> *Me: You might just be right about that. Maybe . . .*

> *Stone: I know I am and all I've been thinking about all day is making you wet again.*

> *Stone: Shit! I can't get my cock to go down. Look what you're doing to me today.*

> *Stone: [dick pic]*

Excitement courses through me as I stare at the picture,

looking at the shape of his hard dick through his jeans.

I seriously can't stop looking.

Why is it so damn big?

> *Stone: Surprised I could fit the whole thing in the screen? Me too.*

> *Me: Why did you have to send me a dick pic? Are you trying to corrupt me?*

> *Stone: With my dick. Yes . . .*

> *Stone: It's the best weapon I have.*

> *Me: It is kind of your best feature ;)*

> *Me: Although I do kind of like your mouth too. It's pretty dirty.*

> *Stone: Kind of? *laughs**

I stare at my phone with a smile, realizing just how much I want get out of the house and see him right now.

Earlier, I was completely exhausted and ready to sleep the day away, but after texting with Stone; I'm wide awake and ready to have some fun.

Gathering something cute to wear, I jump into the shower and quickly redo my hair and makeup, before I can change my mind.

When I look down at my phone, I have two new messages from Stone, ten minutes apart.

> *Stone: Still hard . . .*

> *Stone: Shit! Some old lady keeps looking at my junk like she*

wants to gum me. Would you think less of me if I admit that I'm scared? She won't stop eye raping it and I need at least one of my hands to serve drinks. I need two to cover it. Well you know that . . .

Laughing, I toss my phone into my purse and grab for my keys, before speed walking to my truck and jumping in.

Looks like Stone might just need a bodyguard right now . . . Or better yet . . . someone to laugh at him.

chapter FOURTEEN

STONE

I'VE BEEN TRYING REALLY HARD for the last twenty minutes, to pretend that *Blanche* hasn't been sitting at the end of the bar, sucking on her straw and watching my every move as if she wants to eat me for a late night snack.

Damn, that woman can drink fast.

And with my luck, the bar has been slow for a Monday night, so not many other women are occupying the seats to keep my ass busy.

"Over here, you cute young thing." She holds up her now empty glass, smiling as I make my way over. "My glass is empty *again*."

"You're really keeping me busy tonight."

She gives me a seductive look and does this weird little old lady dance in her seat. "Oh, I like keeping you busy and watching you work with those tight little buns."

I give her my best smile, blocking out the fact that she's now showing even more cleavage than she was the last three times I poured her a drink. "I'll take it," I say to be polite, while pouring her a new drink.

She leans in to get closer, her hand coming up to cover mine as I slide her glass in front of her. "Oh my." She bites her bottom lip and smiles. "Your hands are so strong." Her eyes lower back down to my jeans. "I wonder what else is strong."

A whistle from the other side of the bar has me mentally doing a victory dance and rescuing my hand from the ninja grip she now has on it.

"Hey! Over here, Bartender. How about you make me that drink that I didn't get to finish last night."

A smile spreads over my face at the sound of her sweet, yet sexy voice.

"Unless you're too busy over there. You look busy. I could find a waitress if you want."

Laughing, I hold my finger up to *Blanche* and excuse myself as quickly as possible.

"You better fucking not," I say with a grin, while walking over to her. "Unless you want me to punish you with my cock later."

Her eyes widen and I think I even notice her cheeks turn a little pink. "Always using your penis as a weapon. Is that all you got?"

She's challenging me. I fucking love it.

After pouring her a drink, I lean in closer. Close enough so my lips are hovering over hers. "I've got my lips." I gently brush them against hers. "And my tongue." She lets out a soft moan as I run my tongue over her bottom lip and growl. "Want to see what I can do with my teeth next?"

Backing away, she shakes her head, while trying to hold back her smile. "What if I say no?"

I watch as she grabs her drink, taking a small sip. "Then I'd say you're lying."

"What's Stone lying about? That his dick is bigger than mine? I'll let you look again for yourself and see."

"Fuck off, Kash."

Kash is standing beside Sage, half-naked and dripping with sweat. Smiling, he turns to face her and points down at his white briefs. "Go ahead, Babe. Look."

Sage smiles and reaches out as if she's going to pull out the waist of his underwear and look, but then stops and shakes her head. "I've already seen all I needed to see."

"What does that mean?" Kash asks, sounding worried. "It wasn't even hard all the way. That shit doesn't count."

I smirk. "Yeah, well she's seen mine halfway hard too, Fucker. She has enough to compare it to."

Sage shrugs. "I'll let you boys figure that shit out on your own."

I don't need to figure shit out. I can tell by the look on Sage's face and the way that her eyes keep lowering to my dick, that she's more impressed with my bulge than his.

Kash's dick is the last thing I worry about.

"Don't you have a show to put on or some shit?"

Kash places his hand behind his head and does a little thrust for Sage, until she pulls out a five-dollar bill and shoves it into the band of his briefs.

"I'm good to go now." Winking, he backs away, almost getting away from the bar, until *Blanche* seeks him out and calls him over.

I watch, laughing with Sage, as she pulls out some money and motions for him to turn around so she can see his ass.

"I thought you might've needed some rescuing from your last text."

"Oh, yeah. Is that why you're here?"

She nods her head. "Of course. What kind of *friend* wouldn't want to see this?"

I laugh and lean over the bar. "It was the dick pic, wasn't it?" I tilt my head. "Was it the outline of the head or the thickness of the shaft that got you rushing here to see me?"

Smiling, she grips the back of my hair and leans in close to my mouth. "It was all of it." She sucks my bottom lip into her mouth, before quickly releasing it. "Now hopefully *that* will have you rushing home to see me."

With a confident grin, she stands up, shoves money down the front of my jeans and backs away to leave.

"Well fuck . . ." I groan, while pushing down on my erection and watching her walk away. "What time is it?"

I look up at the clock to see that I still have four more fucking hours until I get out of here tonight.

"Fuck me!"

***

KASH AND STYX HAVE SPENT the last hour hanging out at the bar, goofing off and having a few drinks.

"Fuck . . . I love it when we get a few minutes of quiet to just enjoy a few drinks, without someone tugging on our balls or dick," Styx says, while taking a swig of his third beer and chillin'.

"I agree, Brother. As much as I love women, my dick needs a break once in a while." Kash tosses a straw my way, hitting me on the shoulder. "What the fuck are you doing over there? Jerking off or some shit?"

"Nah, Fucker." I hold my phone out, being sure to get the whole length in the camera. It's not an easy task and that's not me being a cocky ass. It's the truth. "Just taking a selfie."

Styx bursts out laughing. "You're taking dick pics and shit over there in the corner. What the fuck. How are you even hard?

There aren't even any women here."

I put my shit away and adjust it on my thigh, before walking over to join them. "The power of the mind, Motherfucker. I know what's at home waiting for me and I'm horny as shit."

Kash watches me as I begin wiping down the bar, preparing for close. I'm just ready to get the hell out of here already. "So you two are at it again?" He smiles as if remembering something. "I'm going home with your ass tonight. I haven't had a good jerk since the showers."

"You fucked Sage in the showers? Damn . . . I missed it," Styx says, looking sincerely disappointed. "Where the hell was I?"

"Not in the next shower over," Kash answers with a cocky grin.

"Since when the hell are women allowed in the back?" Styx takes another swig of his beer. "I tried sneaking one in and Kass jumped down my throat and shit."

"They're not." I toss the dirty towel at him. He just frowns and pushes it away. "Looks like Kage was too busy working on getting pussy, than guarding the door."

"So distracting the big guys does the trick." Styx stands up and tosses some money my way for his drinks, knowing damn well I hate when one of the guys tries tipping me. "Noted."

Wadding up his cash, I toss it at the back of his head when he begins walking away. "Not picking it up," he grumbles. "See ya, Dicks."

Kash looks at me and then down at the wadded up money. "Fuck you both. I'll take it then."

Finishing up my shit, I shake my head as Kash picks it up and shoves it in his pocket. "Now get the hell out of here so I can. Go find Kane and see if he's out of the shower so I can lock up. If not, tell him to hurry the hell up. I swear he takes the longest fucking showers."

"Got it."

I'm seriously going crazy to get the fuck out of here and get home to Sage. The things I've been imaging doing to her body has made being here painful as shit.

She hasn't been this playful since we stopped talking months ago and I have to admit that it makes me happy. All of me.

I'm taking this side of Sage while she's willing to give it and doing everything in my power to keep her this way.

If it takes my body to keep her for now, I'll take it and work as hard as I can to keep her emotionally later.

Damn . . . I hope she's still awake when I get home.

chapter FIFTEEN

STONE

WHEN I GET HOME, I search through the house to find it empty. Her car's here in the driveway, so I check the last possible place she can be, knowing that she must be outside on the balcony.

Sliding the glass door open, I smile down at her sleeping in one of the lounge chairs, with a half-empty glass of wine, setting on the table beside her.

I find it really fucking cute that she fell asleep waiting on me to get home. Now I really need to make it worth her while.

She's usually sleeping by the time I get home, but never out here, with a glass of wine with music playing from her iPod.

Turning the music up, I smile when *Pillow Talk* from Zayn comes through the speakers. The part about pissing off the neighbors might be happening tonight.

Lowering myself to the lounge chair, I straddle her lap, brush the hair away from her ear and whisper her name, causing her to make this cute little whimpering noise.

"Stone," she says tiredly. "What time is it?"

Ignoring her question, I grab her hands and place them on my chest as I begin grinding on her lap to the music.

Her lips instantly twitch up into a smile as I begin to slowly lower her hands down my body and to my abs.

She begins fingering the dips of my muscles and reaching for the bottom of my shirt to lift it. She's still half asleep so she struggles with it.

"Take it off," she whispers. "Wake me up."

Smirking, I rip my shirt off from over my head and grab both ends of it, placing it behind her neck for support as I begin grinding harder in her lap.

Biting her bottom lip, she reaches for my belt and undoes it, before slowly ripping it from the loops of my jeans, while I move for her.

Her eyes widen when she goes for my jeans, noticing that I'm not wearing anything underneath. "Jeez, Stone. Do you even own underwear anymore."

I toss my shirt aside. "I find that I don't need them much these days."

Sitting up on my knees, I lower my fitted jeans down past my hips, allowing my hard cock to plop out in front of her.

I stroke my hand up and down it a few times, before raising it up high enough for my cock to brush against her lips.

Grabbing me by the balls, she pulls me closer and swipes her tongue out to twirl it around the piercing in my dick.

She does it a few more times, before I reach for her shirt, pulling it off over her head. Her plump tits plop out, her nipples instantly perking up for me.

Lowering myself down her body, I take her right nipple into my mouth, swirling my tongue around the piercing, just as she did to the one in my dick.

Her hands reach up to grab at my hair.

This turns me on even more. Especially when she pulls it, hard.

"Damn you . . ." she moans out as I kiss her stomach and slowly start lowering my mouth to beneath the waist band of her cotton shorts. "Your mouth feels good on my body. Why are you so good at this?"

I smile against her smoothly waxed mound. "Because I take pride in making sure that I can pleasure you better than anyone else can."

Trailing my tongue down her body, I slowly pull her shorts and underwear down to give me access to her wet pussy.

The moment my tongue presses against her clit, she grips my hair and moans loudly. "Holy . . . fuck . . ."

Her moaning becomes louder and louder with each flick and swirl of my tongue.

I lick and suck her for as long as I can take it, before I pull her up to her feet and bend her over the balcony.

"Hold on tight. Fuck . . . this is going to be rough."

I reach into my jeans for a condom, before stepping out of them and kicking them aside.

We're both out here on the balcony completely naked and turned on, not giving a shit who we might disturb.

Fuck it. Let them watch.

Roughly, grabbing the back of her hair, I tangle my hand in it and pull as I slam into her.

She screams out in a mixture of pleasure and pain, while gripping even harder onto the balcony.

With my free hand, I lift her left leg up and hold it, while I continue to thrust and grind my hips, pounding into her as deeply as I can.

She moans and cries out with each hard thrust, letting me know how much she enjoys taking my cock.

I can't be gentle. Not tonight.

I want her to still feel me tomorrow. I want her to remember how hard and deep I took her tonight.

My grip on her hair tightens as I slow down and pull out, before thrusting back in, taking her breath away.

"Oh shit . . ." she breathes out, sounding as if she's fighting to catch her breath.

I pull out again and slam into her as hard as I can. "Let the neighbors know my name," I growl out. "I want them to know how good I feel inside of you. Show them."

Pulling her neck back so I can bite her neck, I pound into her fast and hard.

So fucking fast and hard that all you can hear now is the slapping of our bodies and her screaming out my name.

"Stone!" Her arm comes behind her to snake around my neck and hold me close as I bite her harder and continue to pound her tight pussy. "Oh shit . . . oh shit. Stone!"

She moans my name on her release and I feel her pussy tightly clamp around my dick as she comes.

There's no doubt in my mind that we've woken up at least one or two of the neighbors. But with my release . . . we might just wake them all.

Pushing into Sage as hard and deep as her body will allow me, I yell out, "Fuck," as loud as I can, while I release my load inside of her, filling up the condom.

Knowing that she likes it when I fuck her with my cum in the condom, I slowly thrust in and out a few more times, while reaching out to rub her clit.

It doesn't take her long, before she's shaking in my arms, gripping at her hair as she has another orgasm.

Holding her tightly, I wait for her to come down from her release, before I pull out of her and kiss the back of her neck.

"Holy fuck, we were loud." I laugh beside her ear.

She lets out a breathy laugh. "You think!" She throws her hand over her mouth and gets all embarrassed when she notices the neighbor's lights are now on next door. "Oh my God."

Laughing, I pull her into my arms and cup her face. "I'm pretty sure neighbors from two blocks over heard you screaming. Don't be ashamed. It was fucking hot."

She playfully slaps my chest and backs away to gather her things. "I should've known better than to wait for you outside. You'll fuck anywhere and in front of anyone, won't you?"

I bite my bottom lip and growl. "Do you even have to ask that?"

"No." She opens the sliding door and stops to look back at me. "Thanks."

I smile back, while pulling off the condom. "For what?"

She motions at my dick. "For having a magic dick." She winks. "Goodnight, Stone."

Feeling good about tonight, I stand back and watch her disappear into the house.

I take a few minutes to just stand outside and enjoy the fresh, night air, before making my way inside myself.

Sage stays on my mind throughout my whole twenty-minute shower, all the way up until my head hits my pillow and I pass the fuck out.

Damn . . . that woman is everything I want.

chapter SIXTEEN

Sage

IT'S BEEN THREE DAYS SINCE our little show on the balcony and I still get embarrassed every time I see one of our neighbors outside when I leave the house.

I swear the seventeen-year-old from the house left of ours has been staring extra hard whenever he sees me now. He might've even smirked a little when we made eye contact before I left for work this morning.

If the kid's going to learn from someone, might as well be Stone, I suppose. Doesn't make it any less embarrassing though, knowing that he was probably getting his rocks off to us.

I'm in the back of the salon, finishing up my lunch, when Aspen pokes her head in the door. "There's a guy out here that wants his hair cut."

I hold up my chicken sandwich. "Alright . . . Why are you telling me? I'm not even on the clock. Can't Onyx take him?"

She gives me a small smile. "I don't know who the cute guy is, but he came in asking for *you* to cut his hair. Is there something

I don't know about? Is that why . . ."

"No," I cut in. "I'm not *seeing* anyone. Trust me, if I was, I'd want a guy like Stone."

Her smile widens. "Good to hear. Hopefully you heard yourself as loud and clear as I did." She backs away. "I'll tell him you'll be out in a few. Take your time."

I nod my head as she closes the door and then quickly finish my lunch, before checking my phone.

My stomach fills with butterflies when I see two missed texts from Stone. I don't know what he's been doing to me lately, but the idea of him excites me more than ever.

Stone: I'm off at eight tonight. Come to Fortunes with us.

Stone: [ab pic]

The picture of Stone holding his shirt up, to flash his abs has me smiling.

He's been on this kick lately of sending me random pictures of his body parts. He even sent one of his ass the other day. Or at least what he could manage to get in the pic.

Me: Very impressive . . . much better than the ass pic you attempted the other day. So about tonight. Who's us?

Stone: Was my ass pic not good enough for you? I can ask Styx to take it for me this time ;)

Stone: Styx and Sara.

I definitely can't say no to that. I never see Sara go out, other than at *W.O.S* and I've been dying to go out with her wild ass. She's been working with the boys for so long, that I'm pretty sure they rubbed off on her.

Me: I'm in . . . and tell Styx I want that pic ;) He can send me one of his too. I wouldn't mind . . .

Stone: He won't be able to if his phone is broken. Mine definitely won't be though . . .

Tossing my wrappers in the trash, I clock back in and make my way out to the front with a laugh.

I'm surprised to see Knight sitting in my chair, waiting on me. My laughter instantly turns into confusion.

Why the hell would he be looking for me?

Onyx gives me a hard look as I walk past her to get to my station. I know how she feels about me giving Stone a chance. The last thing I need is for her to think I'm into some other guy.

Far from it.

The only guy I've been into for the last year is Stone. Who happens to be my brother's close friend and the coolest, sweetest guy I've ever met.

So basically, the last guy I want to hurt or mess up my brother's friendship with. That's why it's so hard to give him everything I know he deserves.

What if I'm just not good at loving someone? I've spent most of my life keeping everyone at a distance so they couldn't hurt me like my deadbeat parents did. They left without caring what happened to Hemy or myself. What if it's just as easy for me to leave someone that I'm supposed to love and hurt them? Or easy for them to leave me.

I have to keep that in mind when it comes to Stone. He doesn't deserve to have his heart ripped out like I have. So that's why I have to make sure he doesn't give it to me; someone that wouldn't even know what to do with it.

Knight looks up at me with a cocky grin, once he notices that I'm now standing next to him.

"I was hoping I'd catch you working today, Beautiful." Sitting up straight, he runs his hands through his hair and looks in the mirror. "I need a quick trim before tonight. Ran into your friend the other day and she gave me your card. Said you're really good."

Good to fucking know . . . Jade.

"I try my best," I say, trying to keep the conversation light. "Are you fighting again tonight?"

His smile broadens in the mirror. "No, I was hoping to get you to come out with me and my friends tonight. I want to make up for my drunken friend acting a fool the other week. He was just really excited for me."

"Thank you, but I can't." I offer him a smile in the mirror, before concentrating back on his hair. "I have plans for tonight."

He looks a little confused at me turning him down. I have a feeling hot MMA fighters don't get turned down very often. Especially ones as well known and popular as himself.

"Maybe you can change them." He reaches out and grips my thigh, when I walk around to get the front of his hair. "I promise it'll be worth it."

His rough grip, causes a small surge of excitement to rush through me, but nothing compared to Stone's touch. Knight might be sexy, strong and highly desired with his fangirls, but he's not getting lucky with me.

Grabbing his hand, I push it away. "No, I'm good."

I let out a small yelp, surprised when he reaches out and grips my ass with both hands, pulling me between his legs in the chair. "Come on, Girl. I saw the way you were checking me out that night. I'm offering you a night out with me. You might not get this opportunity again."

Smiling, I lean in to whisper in his ear. "I don't know. I need to test something out first." Gripping his package, I squeeze as hard as I can and twist, causing him to cuss and grip the chair. "You can't handle a woman like me. Now keep your hands to yourself for the rest of your cut or I'll rip it off next time. Got it?"

When I let go, he looks me up and down, smiling as if I've only just turned him on more.

"Oh fuck." He throws his hands up. "You're tougher than some of the guys I fight. That's so hot."

Pulling at his head, I hold him still so I can get his fucking hair cut and kick him out of here, before I lose it.

"You're really just not used to being told no, are you?" I ask stiffly.

He smiles up at me in the mirror. "Fuck no. You're the first. Most girls love being handled by me. It comes with being a fighter I suppose. You're different."

"I'm not that easy, playboy and I'm definitely not one of your fighter groupies."

He bites his bottom lip and silently watches me the whole time I'm cutting his hair.

Standing up, he follows me over to the counter to pay for his cut. "Hopefully I'll see you around." He winks at me and then walks out the door.

When I turn around, both Aspen and Onyx are looking at me.

"I was so close to sticking my heel in that asshole's neck. He's lucky you handled him and not me."

I definitely agree there. Onyx is one crazy bitch when it comes to protecting her friends and family. Mess with her and there's a high possibility you could end up with a shoe sticking out of your neck. Just as she said.

"I almost kicked his ass out," Aspen joins in, "But I know how you are about not letting some asshole feel like you're weak. So I left it up to you to handle first. He won't be allowed back in though. Fuck that. He's done."

I shake my head in disbelief that he even showed up here in the first place. "I'm sure he won't be coming back anyway. He's got plenty of other girls that are too willing to jump into bed with an asshole like him."

When I make it back over to my station to clean, I notice a crisp, black business card with his info, laying in the seat.

"Wow. Seriously." I rip the card up and toss it into the trash.

"Some men," Onyx mumbles. "They're fucking idiots when it comes to women. Not Stone though."

"I agree," Aspen jumps in, smiling at me. "How's that going, by the way? Slade said you and Stone have been keeping the whole neighborhood up at night."

"What the fuck!" Onyx yells. "You guys are back to fucking and I didn't even know? Wild sex too, apparently. Sounds fun."

"Slade has a big mouth and apparently, so does Stone. I don't know what to do with these fucking men."

"Love them," Onyx says. "It's all we can do. They're a fucking handful, but they're beautiful as sin and know how to keep us satisfied."

Just then my phone vibrates in my pocket. I pull it out to see three texts from Stone.

Stone: *I had to hunt Styx down for this ;)*

Stone: *[ass pic]*

Stone: *Styx's phone is broken. The fucker was going to send you a dick pic.*

I agree. Stone is definitely beautiful as sin and a master at pleasing me. Too good, actually. And he knows damn well too. Damn him and that sexy ass of his . . .

chapter
SEVENTEEN

STONE

I TAKE A SHOWER AT the club and head straight for *Fortunes*, knowing that Sara and Sage are already there, waiting on me to show up.

Styx has one more private dance before he can get away from *W.O.S* so I told him to just meet us after he cleans up.

The last thing I wanted to do was waste time waiting on that fucker, just so I'd get stuck seeing his ass run around the locker room naked like usual.

I've seen enough of that asshole's dick to last me a lifetime.

Plus, Sage messaged me about thirty minutes ago, letting me know they showed up early. My plan was to go home first, but there's no way I'm leaving the ladies there alone for longer than I have to, so I'm pulling into the parking lot now.

Jumping out of my jeep, I smooth out my black V-neck and adjust my dick in my jeans the best I can so that it's not the first thing every woman notices when I walk by.

Apparently, I've already used all of my extra boxer briefs that

I had stored in my locker and there was no fucking way I was throwing my sweaty ones back on after I showered.

I'm going commando.

When I walk through the door, the waitress walking by flashes me a huge smile after looking up from my crotch.

So much for the big guy not getting noticed . . .

Standing in the darkened room, I search for Sage and Sara to find them in the back corner, laughing about something.

Sara notices me first and starts waving me over, while listening to whatever it is that Sage is focused on at the moment.

Keeping my eyes on Sage, I make my way over, smiling as she finally looks up at me, looking happy to see me standing beside her.

"Someone's looking mighty fine tonight. I've always thought black was your color." She winks, but then her eyes widen as they lower down my body, landing on the bulge in my pants. "Seriously? You can see *everything* and I do mean *everything*. You're not at the club, Stone."

Shrugging, I grab the beer they have waiting for me and take a swig of it. "Didn't have time to run home. Which might fucking suck since you look so damn hot right now. There's no way I'm going to be able to keep my dick in control."

Sara smiles and stands up to get a look of her own. "Damn, Stone. You're really not leaving much for the imagination. I love it."

"That's because you're dirty minded as fuck," I point out with a grin.

"True. What can I say. I've been working with you boys for too long."

Sage laughs against her drink. "Where's Styx?"

"Finishing up a private dance. He'll be here soon."

"Hopefully with underwear," she teases. "Not sure we can

keep the waitresses away with you both going commando." She looks down at my jeans again, as if she can't help but to look. She bites her bottom lip and reaches for her drink again. "I need to thank him for that photo you sent me earlier."

"What photo?" Sara perks up. "Are you guys getting freaky and I don't know about it?" She holds her hand out. "Gimmie."

"You would ask too." Sage pulls out her phone with a laugh and holds it out for Sara to look.

"Very nice ass." Sara whistles. "Zoom in a bit. I've seen it at the club, but not up this close. Dayum."

"Hey, I made Styx look at it. Might as well let Sara see my magnificent ass too. Zoom that shit in."

"Dude, not with your fucking ass again." Styx pulls up a seat, squeezing his way in between the girls. "You ladies are looking fucking hot tonight."

"I thought you had a private dance?" I ask while watching him place his arms around the girls as if his ass thinks he's taking one of them home tonight.

Fuck that. There's no way Sage is going anywhere near his place.

"She was a fast one. Took one look at my hard dick and came." He lifts a brow with a cocky ass grin.

"It must've been the first dick she's seen."

Grabbing the bottom of Sage's chair, I pull her over to me and away from Styx, before he can even think for one second that he has a chance.

Styx flashes me the middle finger and waves the waitress over to order the whole table a round of drinks. "What can I say . . . Sage can see for herself."

He winks as Sage's phone goes off on the table. Before I can snatch it up, Sara has it in her hand with her mouth hanging open.

"Holy fuck, you're hung, Styx. Damn, your dick is perfect. Look, Sage."

"Seriously, Fucker. I thought your phone was broken." I shrug as he holds his phone out for Sage to see. "That's the closest your dick's getting to her face so enjoy, Asshole."

Sage's eyes widen a bit as she gives Sara a nod of agreement. "Not bad, Styx. Definitely not bad."

"Damn straight. My dick is sexy as fuck."

After a few rounds of drinks, everyone's laughing and having a good time, but all I can think about is how hot it would be to have Sage's hand around my cock right now.

She's been trying to play if off, but every once in a while, I catch her looking down at it and biting her bottom lip.

I lean into her ear and grab her hand. "You can touch it," I whisper. "You can do anything you want to me."

Pulling her chair even closer, I place her hand on my lap and let her do the rest.

Responding to something that Sara asked her, she smoothly glides her hand over my thigh, rubbing her hand over the shape of my dick.

It instantly gets hard under her touch, causing her to grip it, hard and smile in satisfaction.

Sara doesn't seem to notice anything going on under the table, but Styx's eyes seem to keep lowering as if he knows that Sage is playing with my cock.

"Are you playing with Stone's dick under the table?" He smirks and places Sara's hand on his thigh. "That's not fair if I'm not getting the same treatment from Sara over here."

Sara punches his arm and laughs. "Not tonight, nipples. I have a date later. Wouldn't want to be thinking about you and your sexy dick if I end up getting laid."

"Why not?" Styx questions, while scooting closer to her to

give her easy access. "It might help you get off harder."

Sage runs her thumb over the head of my dick, before pulling her hand away and reaching for her drink. "Yeah, well Sara's date is actually pretty hot. She showed me a picture."

Styx lets out a huff. "I doubt that fucker's hotter than I am."

Sara pushes her chair away from his and rests her legs in his lap. "Give me a leg rub and I'll think about taking you home one of these nights."

He smiles and grabs her legs, pushing them down so she can feel the bulge in his pants. Then he begins moving his hips. "How's this? All I have to use is my dick."

Sara shrugs and grabs her drink. "I'll take it. Something as sexy as *that* has to be talented."

Ignoring those two goofing off, I place my hand at the back of Sage's neck and pull her in for a kiss, while placing her hand back on my dick.

Other guys keep looking her way, checking her out, but there's no way in hell I'll be letting any of them get close to her.

This is me letting them know who she belongs with. The only place she'll be going tonight, is home, to our place.

Her kiss is soft, her mouth instantly parting for me to slip my tongue inside and capture hers.

Kissing her harder, my hand tangles into the back of her hair, wanting to get as close to her as I can right now.

I'm trying really hard to not get carried away, but I can't help it when it comes to Sage.

I'm just about to pull her into my lap, when both Styx and Sara begin whistling really loud and trying to get our attention.

"Hello! This nice waitress here is trying to offer us shots," Sara says while sliding two shots across the table to us. "And you two are over there practically about to have sex. Break it up."

Pulling away from me, Sage reaches for the shot in front of

her and slides mine closer to me, while wiping her finger over her lips to wipe her smeared lip gloss off.

Thanking the waitress, I pull out some cash and place it on her tray, before we all slam our shots back and fall into conversation.

I catch Sage's eyes keep going over to a certain part of the room, so I follow them to see what she's now looking at.

Fucking Knight Stevens.

Watching her, I can't help but to notice her looking uncomfortable all of a sudden. It's almost as if she wants to get out of here.

"What's wrong?" I question, while gripping her thigh. "Did that asshole do something to you?"

"Doesn't matter." Looking flustered, she takes another sip of her drink and focuses on looking anywhere but at him. "I took care of it."

Feeling my blood boil in anger, I quickly finish my beer off, before slamming it down on the table.

That gets Knight's attention, causing him to smirk my way from his spot up at the bar now.

"That fucker's dead."

Before Sage can say anything to stop me, I'm walking across the room to where Knight is standing at the bar.

One of his friends try to stand in my way, but I shove him into a table, letting the fucker know I'm not playing. He throws his arms up and gets out of my way.

"You fuck with my girl?"

Knight laughs, clearly drunk this time and not thinking straight. A male stripper kicking his ass will be bad as shit for his reputation. "I think she liked it. She did grab my dick afterward."

Stepping in front of Knight, I swing my elbow out hard, connecting it with his jaw. Then I grab the back of his head, slamming it into the side of the bar.

I rotate my shoulders in anger as I look down at him, waiting for him to get up. "Get up, you piece of shit."

Standing up, he looks down at the blood on his shirt, before wiping his thumb under his nose. "You really want to do this? You do know I could probably kill your ass, right? Or are you going to hip thrust my ass like the male fucking entertainer that you claim to be."

"Fuck you."

He swings out, his fist connecting it with my nose.

I wipe my nose off and tilt my head, tensing my jaw at him. Seeing red, I swing my right fist, connecting it with the fucker's jaw.

He stumbles back, but quickly regains his balance, slamming me into a nearby table, knocking all of the drinks over.

My back gets wet, but that's the last thing on my mind. This asshole did something to Sage and I'm not letting that shit ride.

I let him get his punch in a few times, before I take control, grabbing him by the neck and slamming him down to the ground.

My fists continue to swing, connecting with his face, until I'm being dragged away from the fight by someone.

It's Styx, who punches some asshole in the side of the head, that tries to push him out of the way.

"What the fuck?" he growls at me, when he releases me. "You could've warned me first."

By the time I look behind me, Knight is back to his feet, pushing and yelling at his guys that are trying to help him.

"Leave me the fuck alone!" He fixes his shirt and punches the table, pissed off that I had to be pulled from him.

"Yeah, well it couldn't wait." I make my way back over to Sage who is looking completely shocked at what I just did. I toss some money on the table, before grabbing her hand. "Let's get out of here."

Styx places his hand on Sara's back and follows us outside to the parking lot.

Sage is the first to speak.

"I can't believe that just happened. I didn't want you to get into a fight for me, Stone."

"Doesn't matter," I say stiffly. "No one fucks with you. You couldn't have stopped me if you tried."

Sara looks down at her watch and cusses. "I'm sorry, but my date starts soon. I need to go, but you will be explaining this shit to me later." She turns to Styx who is still fuming. "Are you good to drop me off? I don't think I should drive."

If anyone can handle their liquor; it's Styx. I'm not sure if the dude ever actually gets drunk. He cuts himself off at a buzz when he knows other people will be drinking.

"Yeah, I'll drop you off." He turns to me. "I'm stopping by later so we can talk about what just happened. Something set you off and I don't like that shit."

Nodding my head, I turn away, placing my hands against the building and taking a deep breath to compose myself.

Sage says her goodbyes to Sara and Styx, before calling for a taxi.

She slides her way in between me and the building, grabbing my face and gently kissing me on the lips. "I don't like you fighting, but the fact that you did it because you care means a lot."

"I'll never let anyone hurt you, Sage," I say with honesty. "I want you to tell me if anyone ever does. Not knowing what he did to you made me see red."

Sliding my hands down from the building, I cup her face. "What did he do?"

She grabs my arms and looks up at me. "He came into the

salon and tried picking me up. He grabbed my ass and I about ripped his dick off. He got the picture. At least I hoped."

The thought of him grabbing her ass, causes more anger to flood through me, but I fight it off, knowing that it will lead me back into the bar, swinging.

"Well he definitely got it now," I growl out. I look over my shoulder when I hear a car pull up. "The taxi's here." I kiss her on the forehead. "Let's get you home."

This asshole is lucky Styx was there to pull me off. Next time he won't be so lucky . . .

STONE

THE BACON SIZZLING, HAS ME rushing from the toaster, back over to the stove before it burns.

"Owe, fuck!" *That shit hurts.*

I knew there was a reason why I stopped cooking bacon. Bacon grease hurts like a bitch when it pops you in the face.

Getting the bacon under control, I quickly whip up some eggs—over easy—like she eats them and slide them onto a plate.

It's been a while since I've cooked Sage breakfast, but after last night, all I've been able to think about are the ways that I can take care of her.

Which led me to waking my ass up at the ass crack of dawn and thawing out some bacon for breakfast.

After everything's cooked and plated up, I push her bedroom door open and walk in to see her sleeping, with the covers kicked down to her feet.

She's sleeping in a thong and that little sheer top that I love so damn much on her. There's only one way I can think about waking her up right now and that involves my face in her sexy, round ass.

There's a huge chance that she might kick my ass afterward, but it'll be worth the risk.

Carefully, crawling into the bed behind her, I lean down and bite her ass cheek, holding her down with my hands.

She instantly begins screaming and squirming in my arms as I continue to gently bite her ass, teasing her.

"Stop!" She begins slapping at me and laughing, while trying to get away from me. "Oh my God! It tickles. It tickles. Holy shit! Stop!"

Laughing against her ass, I bite her one last time, just to work her up, before slapping her ass and releasing her, allowing her to flip around to face me.

As soon as she does, she tackles me down to the bed and straddles me, holding my arms down. "I should so kick your sexy ass right now."

Smiling, I free my arms from her hold and grip both of her ass cheeks, placing her roughly on my dick. "So you're saying you'll be aggressive with me."

I flex my dick, causing it to move beneath her. It's hard as shit now and I want nothing more than to skip breakfast and treat her to something else.

Giving me a dirty little smile, she slowly moves down my body as if she's working her face down toward my dick. Her mouth opens to bite the band of my sweats as if to pull them down with her teeth, but then she stops and sniffs the air with a playful smile. "Mmm . . . what's for breakfast."

Giving my dick a hard bite, through my sweats, she slaps my chest and jumps off of me to run out of the room.

"Dammit," I whisper to myself.

Jumping out of her bed, I push down on my erection and

make my way into the kitchen to see Sage already seated at the table, shoving bacon into her mouth.

"Soooo good," she mumbles around her food. "I almost forgot how good you are at cooking breakfast. What do I need to do to get this kind of treatment more often?"

I smile. "Sleep in that sexy little outfit and kick the blanket down at night. It might also help to keep the door open so I can creep."

"Ha! And *help* you creep. That's just too easy on your part."

"You might just wake up to a surprise." I wink.

Seeing how much she's enjoying her breakfast makes it worth the blue balls that I'll most likely have for the next hour, until I can work my shit out in the shower.

Her happiness is all I'm worried about. I'd do anything to see her smile every day and I'm hoping to show her that.

I take a seat across from her and dig into my own plate. I try to focus on my food, but I can't stop thinking about that asshole trying to fuck with Sage. "What are you doing after work? Going out?"

She looks up from her plate. "I don't know yet. Maybe writing for a bit and then hanging with Jade. Why?"

I shake my head. "Just wondering where you'll be."

"I'm not hanging out with Knight if that's what you're asking. I don't want anything to do with that asshole."

My jaw tenses at his name. "Good. That shit won't be happening as long as I'm still breathing."

"You sound like Hemy." Her mouth turns up into a small, knowing smile. "You boys and your overprotectiveness. I'll never have to worry as long as I have you both."

She gets quiet, as if she's just now realizing what she's said.

It's the fucking truth. I just hope she can see that and stop fighting it.

"Never forget that," I say firmly. "And promise me you'll call me if that asshole ever shows up at the salon again. I'll rip the fucker's throat out."

"I promise, Stone. He won't be coming back. So don't worry." She clears her throat and finishes off her orange juice, before standing. "I need to take a quick shower before work." Grabbing the back of my head, she gently kisses me on the lips, grazing me with her tongue, before she pulls away. "Thanks for breakfast."

"Welcome, Beautiful girl," I whisper as she walks away. "Stop shaking your ass like that. Fuck . . ."

Damn . . . I'm going to need a long shower when she leaves.

I HAVE TWO MORE HOURS before I have to be at the club, so I go to the gym that Styx manages, knowing that he'll most likely be there until our shift starts tonight.

When he's not fucking some random chick in a back room or shaking his dick at *W.O.S*; he's here working out or barking orders at people.

The dude doesn't mess around when it comes to him running the gym for his uncle. Between spending his days here and his nights at the club, I don't know how the fucker ever has any free time.

"What's up, Bro." Styx runs over to me, sweaty and out of breath. "Getting some lifting in before work?"

"Nah, man. Not tonight." I pull out my headphones and toss my gym bag aside. My mind hasn't left Sage all day and running on the treadmill usually helps calm my mind. "Running off some frustration."

Styx laughs, while wiping his sweat off with his shirt. "What, jerking your shit in the shower didn't do the fucking trick?"

"Does it ever really?"

He smirks when some hot chick with pale, purple hair walks by, running her hand across his bare stomach.

"I'll be back. Maybe . . ."

Shaking my head, I put my headphones on and jump on the treadmill, hoping to clear my thoughts.

Every so often, I look up to see a new chick on the treadmills beside me, checking me out and giving me *the* look. Knowing that they'll never satisfy my craving for Sage, I continue to run hard, ignoring them, until they give up and leave.

Getting laid by some random chick, is the last thing on my fucking mind right now.

Stepping off the treadmill, I look around to see if Styx's ass is still around. I haven't seen him since he disappeared over an hour ago.

Our shift starts in less than thirty minutes so I need to find his ass and get him out of here.

I walk around the whole gym, but don't see his ass anywhere, so I look outside for his motorcycle to see it still parked out front. I know the fucker is here somewhere.

There's only one place left he could be.

Not bothering with knocking, I push his office door open to see his naked ass as he pounds into the chick from earlier.

Holding her up against the wall, he thrusts into her hard and deep and then stops. "Fuck . . . your pussy feels good. Nice and wet for me. So tight."

Pulling her away from the wall, he turns around and slams her roughly against his desk, before gripping her neck, choking her.

"Shit," he growls, when he sees me. "Already?"

"Yeah, Fucker. Hurry your ass up."

The hot girl tilts her head back to look at me. "Oh wow." She bites her bottom lip, while looking me over and gripping at Styx's broad shoulders, digging her nails in. "Can your friend here join?"

Styx shrugs, not giving a shit either way. As long as his dick is buried between her legs, he could care less about what she does with her mouth.

"Sorry, Babe." I give Styx a hard look when he begins fucking her again as if I'm not even standing here and shit. "Seriously?"

"Gotta get the job done, Asshole. Just give me five minutes."

"Five minutes and you better run out the fucking door naked with your dick in your hand if you have to. We can't be late."

I back out of the office and shut the door behind me, giving him his time. All I can hear after I'm outside is the girl screaming loudly, and shit being broken. The fucker is rough as shit. Almost scary sometimes, but the women always seem to enjoy it.

Random people around the gym look my way, wanting to know what's happening in the office. I'm not lying for the asshole.

"The dicks getting laid. I'm sure you're all used to it by now," I say, before walking away to gather my shit and wait for him outside.

I'd leave his ass, but I know damn well that Cale would ream my ass if he knew I let Styx be late on one of our busiest nights.

Fucking Styx and his dick. Always finding some way to get in trouble . . .

chapter NINETEEN

Sage

JADE HAS BEEN GOING ON about who knows what for the last hour, but I haven't been able to concentrate on anything other than Stone.

He looked stressed when I left for work this morning and I have a feeling that it was because he's worried about Knight bothering me again.

I sent him a message over an hour ago to let him know that I'm at Jade's house with her, but he hasn't responded to it. For some reason I just want to let him know that I'm safe.

It's a busy night for the club, so I doubt he'll have his phone on him at all tonight.

" . . . long day and I just want to get laid. Is that too much to ask? I work hard, dammit."

I only catch the end of what she says, but the get laid part is a good enough reason for her to agree to what I'm about to suggest.

"Let's go see the boys. That should make your night ten

thousand times better."

Jade perks up, setting her bag of bacon jerky aside. "Now that's a damn good idea." She jumps to her feet. "Let me throw some pants on and brush my teeth."

"Good idea." I laugh as she runs pant less into her room, looking fully awake for the first time since I walked through her door.

"You could've been nice enough to throw on pants before your guest arrived. Just saying."

"I may be nice, but not *that* nice." She grabs for her purse and keys. "Let's go. I'll drive."

Jade smiles the whole way to the club.

"What are you smiling so much about?" I ask, when she parks.

She pulls her keys out of the ignition and turns to me. "We're here to watch the boys. Please do tell me what there isn't to smile about."

She has a point there.

"Gotcha, but tone it down a bit before people think you're crazy or something."

We both laugh.

When we get to the door, Kass is taking IDs. He gives us a wink when he notices us in the crowd. "Get up here, Ladies."

A few of the girls sound their disappointment, but Kass just gives them his heart stopping smile and pulls us up to the front of the line.

"These girls are gonna love us," Jade points out. "Not that I mind one bit." She smiles sweetly. "Thanks, Sweetie."

"Figured you wouldn't," Kass says smoothly. "Get your asses in there."

"What would we do without you boys, Kass?" I grab his hand and wink when he reaches his out to hold mine.

"Go enjoy the show."

He gives me a pat on the butt to get me moving, before turning back to handle the line of women.

Jade grips my arm when we walk in to Styx on the stage, stripping out of a pair of leather pants and biker boots. "Holy motherfucking shit. That man is hawt. Please tell me he owns a motorcycle."

"You're not lying," I agree. "Those pants look delicious on that man's firm ass. I can see why he spends so much time in that gym he manages."

After grabbing some drinks from Sara, we make our way over to a table and quickly look up at the stage to see what everyone is suddenly screaming about.

Styx's leather pants are hanging so low on his hips that the top of his shaft is on display for the hundreds of women in the crowd.

We all watch extra hard as he holds up a bottle of chocolate syrup and squirts it on his abs, moving his body to the slow, seductive rhythm and letting the chocolate slowly run down his body, coating his front.

Tossing the bottle aside, he fingers for some girl to enter the stage, before placing his hand on her head and dropping her down to her knees in front of him.

He thrusts his hips close to her face, before demanding her to lick the syrup from his muscles, leading her down lower to his tight abs.

When she's done, she looks up at him as if waiting for instructions on what to do next.

He grabs both of her hands and places them on the waist of his pants, before grabbing her hair and biting his bottom lip as she yanks them down his tatted, muscled legs.

His dick is exposed for a few seconds, causing the women to

scream and throw money at the stage, before he covers himself with both hands and steps completely out of his boots and pants.

He's standing there completely naked now as the chosen girl licks the few last drops of chocolate from his body. And when I say from his body. I pretty much mean the base of his dick that is still exposed to us.

Suddenly, the lights go dark and everyone is left to wonder what the hell happened next. A few girls even gasp and start yelling for the lights to come back on.

I don't need to be told what is most likely going on in the dark. I know without a doubt that Styx probably dropped his hands and let the hot chick finish cleaning off every last drop of chocolate.

For all we know, he could be getting his dick sucked right here on the stage and we just can't see it. I somehow find that to be hot.

"Wow!" Jade bumps my arm and squeals with excitement. "That was really hot. What do you think Stone will do tonight?"

I grab my drink and nervously take a sip. I don't even want to know. Not if it's anything like Styx's performance. "I don't know," I whisper. "But I hope it doesn't involve chocolate."

The thought of some random girl getting to lick chocolate off of Stone's body makes me sick to my stomach.

The only tongue I want on his body is mine. I'm suddenly feeling a bit selfish with him.

The lights come back on after about five minutes of complete darkness and Kash takes the stage next, also dressed in a pair of sexy leather pants.

Then Styx and Kash take the stage together, bringing two girls on stage and sharing, going back and forth.

It's been almost an hour and I haven't seen Stone at all. It reminds me that I didn't even see Stone's jeep when we pulled in.

I figured it was because I just overlooked it. But now . . .

"Have you seen Stone anywhere?" I ask Jade, pulling her attention away from the boys on stage.

"No . . . I almost forgot about him," she responds. "Maybe he's been stuck doing private shows. I'm sure he'll be out soon."

"I don't know." I sit up tall and begin looking around the darkened room, feeling a bit worried that he possibly isn't even here tonight. "I didn't see his jeep outside either."

Setting my drink aside, I pull out my phone to check for a response from him, but nothing.

I anxiously twirl my phone in my hand and begin searching the room again, somehow managing to spot Stone walking out of one of the private rooms as if he's in a hurry.

A few seconds later, three girls walk out of the same room looking completely satisfied at whatever show he just put on in there for who knows how long.

" . . . hey you. You want another drink or what? You've been chewing on that straw for the last ten minutes."

I look down at my empty glass. "Yeah, just a beer this time."

She smiles and holds up her wallet. "I'll be right back. Don't let none of these crazy bitches steal my spot. Some of the girls from the back somehow keep getting closer and closer to the damn stage."

I lift my eyebrows and toss my purse in her seat. "All taken care of. Just hurry!"

The stage darkens after Kash and Styx jump off of the stage and get swallowed up by the herd of horny women.

"Here!" Jade shoves a beer into my hand. "Stone's up next. Sara told me he's been caught up in private dances all night. Poor guy must be exhausted by now."

Earned It by The Weeknd comes through the speakers, before the stage lights up enough to see Stone standing there in a pair of leather pants with suspenders, a black beater and a black fedora hat.

Walking out slowly, he grabs his hat and slowly moves his body to the music, while walking around the stage for the women to get a good view.

Damn . . . he looks fucking great in that.

Then he lowers his body and does this sexy little grind, while lifting the front of his shirt for us.

The way he's grinding his hips even has me dying for him to take it all off.

"Holy shit, Stone." I grip my beer and take a gulp of it, while keeping my eyes on his every move.

His hands move over to his suspenders, playing with the straps as he continues to move, not missing a beat.

With a sexy smirk, he yanks his suspenders to the side, letting them hang, before reaching for his shirt again.

Pulling, he rips it off and tosses it aside, before dropping to his knees and slowly fucking his way across the stage.

Once he gets to where he wants, he sits up on his knees, grabs what looks like a water bottle of some kind, and slowly pours it down the front of his body, while moving his body to the music.

He leans his head back and runs a hand over his wet chest and abs, before grabbing his dick and thrusting his hips.

The women go crazy when he throws the empty bottle into the crowd and undoes his pants to stick his hand down the front.

I scream too, joining in. I can't help it. He has me extremely excited right now.

He makes his way back to his feet, his eyes somehow finding me in the crowd. It must've been my screaming that caught his attention. I guess I was a little louder than I thought.

Giving me his sexy, confident smile, he pulls his hat off and tosses it to the ground, before making his way off the stage and coming right for me.

A few girls reach for him, but he keeps his eyes on me, not taking them off, until he's standing right in front of me.

Grabbing my chair with force, he yanks me into the middle of the aisle and straddles my lap, dancing against me.

Getting lost in the moment, I bite my bottom lip and moan under my breath when he grabs my hands, placing them to his chest and abs as he grinds on me.

Then he does something that completely and utterly surprises the shit out of me and sends my heart soaring.

Grabbing the back of my head, he crushes his lips against mine, kissing me hard and deep as if letting the whole room know that he wants me and doesn't care what they think.

I would've never in a million years expected him to kiss me during a performance, knowing that it could mess up his popularity and high demand here at the club.

But the way he's kissing me feels like more than just a kiss. It feels like he's baring his soul for the world to see. Myself included and I don't know what to do with it.

So I just kiss him back.

My heart continues to beat out of my chest the whole time that our lips mold together, our tongues desperately seeking each other's as if we're alone in the privacy of our home.

When his lips finally separate from mine, he leans in to whisper in my ear. "No one else gets this kind of treatment, Babe." He tangles his hand in my hair and tugs, while breathing heavily against my ear. "The question is . . . what are you going to do with it?"

With that, he stands up and pushes my chair back to the table, before rushing back up to the stage to finish the last part of his routine.

Most of the girls look at me with jealousy, while some of them just look even more excited as if they expect me to just be some random, lucky chick that got a kiss from the sexiest damn stripper that has walked that stage.

You'd have to be blind to think it was just random. He made it extremely clear that he has feelings for me.

Not to mention that he made sure to make it clear that I need to figure out what to do with them.

That thought scares me, yet I can't move from my spot when his show is over.

"You okay," Jade asks. "That boy cares for you. Looks like the whole room knows now too. That kiss was something deep and meaningful. You're lucky, Sage. Stone is a great guy."

"He is. He's the greatest guy I know other than my brother," I whisper, while still lost in thought.

And I want to be here for him when he gets off for the night. I'm not leaving until he does.

Maybe a small part of me does know what to do with it . . .

chapter TWENTY

STONE

"DUDE, WHAT THE HELL WAS that? I still can't get over the shit you pulled out there on the floor," Kash continues to go on about my kiss with Sage. "You do realize that you probably just fucked up your reputation here, right? That kiss was deep, Bro. Real deep. The women won't like that."

I throw my shit into my locker and slam it closed. "Does it look like I give a shit?" I rake my hands through my wet hair in frustration.

The only thing I'm thinking about is what I whispered in her damn ear and how she's going to take it.

There's a huge fucking chance that I've just messed things up with Sage completely and she'll back off, wanting to go back to being strictly roommates again. I can't have it. I won't.

There's no way in hell I'll be able to live with her and not want her like I do every day. I need to see how she truly feels about me. It's been eating at me the more and more that I touch her.

"This job isn't everything, Fuck face. The hundreds of women that grab at me every damn night, begging to take me home to fuck them, will never keep me satisfied for longer than a night. I've been fighting to hold onto Sage for over a year. Do you get that?"

Kash nods his head in understanding and slips a clean shirt on. "I get it, Man. I do. I've been there in the past. I've been hurt and I've moved on, but you still have to think about your career and what you've built here. The women want us to come off as available to them. They want to go home fantasizing that they have a chance with us. It keeps them coming back. That's all I'm saying."

"Get off his fucking ass," Styx grinds out, while stepping out of the shower, completely fucking naked as usual. "Worry about what you do and he'll worry about his own shit. I'd do it in a heartbeat for the right woman. If I ever get lucky enough to fucking find her."

"Fuck off, Styx. I'm just trying to give him some advice and get him thinking straight. I'm down for him winning Sage over as much as you two dicks are. I'm just thinking about the club too."

I throw my dirty clothes into my duffle bag and throw is over my shoulder. "I am thinking straight. I know what I want and I'm going after it at all costs. Fuck the club. Fuck what anyone thinks. She's all that matters. Later, Dickheads."

Not wanting to listen to Kash and his logical fucking bullshit any longer, I hurry out of the locker room and outside toward Hemy's motorcycle.

I borrowed that shit without him knowing, while he took off to work on my jeep earlier. He told me to take his old truck, but I said fuck it and took off on his bike. He hasn't called me yet to kick my ass, but the nights still early. At least for me.

When I walk outside there are still groups of women

hanging outside by the building, checking me out and going on about our performances tonight, but there's one woman in particular that catches my attention and keeps it.

No one else ever seems to exist when it comes to this woman.

Sage is leaning against Hemy's motorcycle, looking lost in thought and slightly confused. She looks torn . . . almost pained.

She's so deep in thought that she doesn't even notice me approaching her.

I hope like hell that it's me she's thinking so hard about right now.

Thankful that she's still here, I wrap my arms around her and pick her up, her legs instantly wrapping around my waist and squeezing.

I flash her a smile, showing her just how happy I am to see her. "Waiting on me, Babe?"

She nods her head and returns my smile. "Yeah, I thought I owed it to you after that amazing kiss that you surprised me with."

"It was pretty amazing." I lift my brows and tangle both of my hands into the back of her hair. "Especially the way you kissed me back. It was sweet and hot as fuck. I haven't stopped thinking about it all night."

Her eyes catch mine and we just look at each other. Like really look at each other for the first time in a long time. Hell . . . maybe even ever. At least on her end.

I take this moment to look into her soul and search for any kind of feelings she might be hiding for me. She may be good at hiding her emotions, but I see something there. Even if it's just something small as hell. It's there. I just need to spark it and make it grow so she can't fight it anymore.

Breaking eye contact, Sage turns her head and clears her

throat, before sliding down the front of my body and fixing her shirt. "Mind if I get a ride, Big guy?"

"Depends on where you're going, Beautiful girl," I tease, while grabbing the helmet and placing it on her head.

"How about for a ride," she says sweetly. "Anywhere. I don't care where. I just want to feel the wind on my face and get lost in my head. I need to get away for a bit."

"I'll take you anywhere you want." It's the honest truth. I care about this woman so damn much that I'll do anything she ever asks of me.

I hop on the front of her brother's bike, before grabbing her hand and helping her on the back. It feels good having her behind me. I really need to invest in one of these bikes my damn self.

We're both quiet as I take off and just drive for a while. I don't give a shit about where we're going or where we end up. Just as long as I'm with her and her arms are wrapped tightly around my waist as if she doesn't want to let go.

Every once in a while, I feel her press her face into my back and squeeze me tighter. My heart speeds up, wondering what she's thinking about. It's almost as if she's taking this as a free moment to hold onto me without any worries of where it might lead us.

We ride for about an hour, with her holding onto me for dear life, until I finally find an open field to park at.

I turn off the engine, but her arms stayed wrapped tightly around me. The last thing I want is for her to leg go, so I spin around on the bike to face her, bringing her up to straddle my lap.

I wrap her arms back around me, before bringing my hands up to cup her face. "How do you feel right now? Don't worry about the future or what could happen. Right here. Right now. What do you feel? What do you want?"

She looks me in the eyes, but hesitates before responding. "It's complicated and completely confusing. I . . . I want to . . . never mind. It's just stupid."

Frustrated, she pulls her face away from my hands, but I capture it again, wanting her to look at me. I never want her to be ashamed to look at me.

"I promise you . . . whatever it is, it isn't fucking stupid. Tell me."

Giving up, she scoots further into my lap and wraps her arms around my neck. "I want to feel what it's like to have you make love to me. Nice. Slow. Passionate. Deep. I just want to experience it once with you and not have to worry about the future."

"Then I'll give that to you," I whisper against her neck. "Anything you want. Ask me and I'll give it to you."

Maneuvering us both off of the bike, I press my lips against hers and carry her over to the grass, gently laying her down in it.

She watches me as I slowly strip out of my clothing, until I'm down to only my briefs.

"You want to do this right here? Right now?" she questions, while looking me over.

"Fuck yes," I growl out. "More than anything."

Spreading her legs, I press my body between them and capture her lips with mine again, tasting her slowly and passionately, wanting her to feel how much she truly means to me.

Moaning softly, she wraps her arms around my neck and lifts her ass up off the ground so that I can pull her jeans and panties down her slender legs. Then, she sits up, allowing me to strip her of her shirt and bra.

Lowering my body, I press kisses down her breasts and stomach, before moving back up to kiss her lips. "If I'm making love to you, I'm doing it without a condom," I say against her lips. "I want you to feel me the right away."

She nods her head. "Okay," she whispers. "I want that too. If I'm going to experience it with anyone . . . I want it to be with you."

Standing up, I pull my boxer briefs down, tossing them aside, before lowering myself back in between her spread legs.

Biting her bottom lip, I slide my hand under her neck and gently guide my hard cock into her pussy. I push into her, moaning as her tightness hugs me completely.

Her body moves with mine, her nails digging into my back as I slowly grind my hips, being sure to hit every spot of pleasure I can find. Hearing her moan and feeling her grip on me tighten, pushes me to want to pleasure her even more. I can never get deep enough when it comes to Sage.

Being inside her this way feels too good emotionally and physically, and I can't help but to feel selfish and only want it to be me from now on. Hell, I'm praying that I've been the only one so far. I can't even imagine this happening with anyone else.

Bringing her legs over my shoulders, I slightly lift her hips and rock into her, biting the side of her calf as I bury myself as deep as I can, causing her to let out a small cry of pain.

"You okay," I whisper.

She nods her head. "Yes," she moans. "Keeping going."

Forty minutes later, both of our bodies are covered in sweat. We're both breathless and completely lost in each other as I continue to thrust deep and slow for what feels like hours.

Wanting to be closer to her, I sit on my knees and bring her body up to straddle my lap. Our bodies are plastered together, not even an inch of breathing room as I kiss her flesh all over and bury myself inside of her over and over again.

I feel her nails dig into my skin and her breathing picks up next to my ear. "I've never felt anything like this before."

Holding her as close as possible, I press my lips to hers and sway my hips, pulling her body so I can get as deep as I can. I feel myself close to orgasm so I suck her bottom lip into my mouth, moaning as she clenches around my cock.

A few seconds later, I rock into her one last time, releasing my load inside of her, being sure that she gets every last drop. I've never come so fucking hard in my life.

She drops her forehead to mine and grabs my face, looking into my eyes as we hold each other. Looking back at her, I feel an emotion rush through me that can hurt us both. Tonight everything is perfect, but what happens when we get back home and she goes back to her room and I get stuck going back to mine.

I don't want that. I want to spend the whole night, holding her in my arms, showing her that it's safe to let me.

We stay still for a while. Ten minutes. Maybe twenty. Doesn't matter. I'll stay here all night, looking at the stars with her, naked, in my lap.

Knowing that she most likely has to be up early though, I kiss her a few more times, before helping her back to her feet and helping her get dressed.

The way she watches me as I gather my own clothing, gives me hope that she wants me to spend the night in her room just as badly as I want to.

"Let's get you home, Beautiful girl."

I secure her with the helmet, just like on the way here, and then help her onto the back of the bike.

Her arms come up to wrap around me, holding me just as tightly as on the way here. Maybe even tighter.

Gives me more hope.

By the time we arrive back at the house, it's close to three in the morning. We're both exhausted, neither one of us jumping to speak.

We both stay quiet as I unlock the door and guide her inside and to her bedroom.

Without a word, I undress us both, before laying her on her bed and crawling in behind her, covering us up with the sheet.

Surprising me completely, she grabs both of my arms, holding me tightly as I rest my face into her neck, getting as close to her as our bodies will allow.

"Goodnight," I whisper.

She doesn't say anything back. Instead, she kisses my arm and buries her face in it.

Fuck . . . please tell me she won't regret this in the morning . . .

chapter
TWENTY-ONE

Sage

FOR THE PAST WEEK, STONE has been crawling into my bed in the middle of the night and catering to my needs as if making me happy and pleasuring me is *his* only need in life.

It's been the best week of my life and the sex has been so intense that it's hard to breathe sometimes when he's inside of me.

The man is so damn good that it makes my heart ache just imagining us going back to how things were a few weeks ago. Back to just friends, when I avoided spending time with him, afraid to get too close.

It also makes my heart ache to imagine what it could be like to allow myself to keep falling deeper and deeper into his world and then have to possibly wake up without him each morning. It's easy to get too used to a good thing and then slowly die from pain and loss when it's no longer in reach.

I remember the feeling all too well, after depending on my brother for love and protection and then to have him ripped away from me without a choice.

I'm not going to lie . . . it scares the living shit out of me. Every day I continue to fall more and more for Stone, losing my strength to fight my feelings for him. It doesn't matter how many times I tell myself that I'm not falling in love with him.

I feel it in my heart and soul.

I find myself wanting to talk to him all day, every day. It's becoming routine to text each other every chance that we get and I find myself waiting for his random pictures to pop up and brighten up my day.

We're beginning to feel more and more like a couple as each day passes and I have no clue how to feel about this or what to do.

"Hey gorgeous, Ladies. Did ya miss me?"

My heart speeds up at the sound of Stone's voice as he enters the salon, greeting, Aspen, Onyx and myself.

"You know it. Us ladies are always happy to see you boys." Aspen smiles as he walks by, kissing her on the side of the head, before he heads over to greet Onyx.

"Hey, Babe. You smell nice." Onyx quickly greets him, trying not to lose focus on her current client. "Tell me what that is later so I can make Hemy buy it."

"I'm sure his ass would love to smell like me," Stone jokes. "Is he still mad about his bike?"

Onyx laughs. "He's over it."

Smiling, he makes his way over to me, wrapping me in his strong arms and kissing me as if it's just so damn natural.

And it is.

Everything about us together just feels natural.

Keeping his arms around me, he picks me up and sets me on my table. "Jesus, you're damn beautiful." He steps between my legs and cups my face. "I wanted to stop in before I head to the club."

My arms instinctively wrap around his neck and pull him closer to me. I can't think when I'm around him. "Mmm . . ." I breathe. "You do smell nice. Sexy. I just want to eat you up."

He pulls my bottom lip into his mouth, roughly biting it, before releasing it. "Don't get my ass worked up right now, Babe. It's bad enough I'll already be wanting to hurry home to see you."

I smile and slap his chest. "I'm nothing special to hurry home to. I'm sure you'll have more fun at the club."

"That's where you're wrong," he says against my lips. "You're very fucking special to me. All I can think about is being close to you. You've ruined me, Sage. Completely."

His words stop my heart and panic sets in.

Swallowing, I quickly kiss him on the lips, before jumping down to my feet. "My client just walked in." I force a smile, pretending with everything in me that his words had no affect on me. "Get your sexy ass out of here before you're late."

"I'll text you when I can." He grabs the back of my neck and firmly places a kiss on my lips. "Stop thinking too hard. Please."

I nod my head and watch him as he walks away. He's so damn beautiful and my eyes can't turn away from his muscled back and legs as he pushes the door open and steps outside.

I instantly feel a loss and my chest aches with need as he hops into his jeep and drives off.

The girls must notice my emotions going everywhere, because they both keep looking over at me with concern.

We don't get time to talk about it for another two hours, when the salon finally quiets down and we get a small break.

"I wish you wouldn't do this to yourself." Onyx walks over and grabs my face, forcing me to look up at her. "I can see your torment over Stone. You love him, don't you?"

Hearing Onyx say it out loud makes it even clearer how

much I truly do love Stone. Maybe I have for a while now.

"I don't know what to do. I'm scared. You saw how I was when you found me in that coffee shop. I was closed off and depressed. If I let Stone in and lose him . . . I'll be devastated."

"Honey," she says softly. "You've already let him in. And it's clear the way he feels about you. I've seen that look before." She smiles. "In Hemy's eyes every damn time he looks at me. I was scared too once. I left Hemy for years and it killed me. I love that man more than life itself and I spend nights thinking about everything I missed from being away from him for so long. You really just need some time to think things over."

"I agree," Aspen jumps in. "I love you and Stone together. I think you guys are truly meant to be together, but if you need time to think, take the time. Truly let your feelings work things out on their own. We're here for you if you need some time."

Onyx gives me a quick kiss and smiles at me. "I love you, Woman. I haven't stopped yet. Give Stone the same faith you've given me since the beginning."

Everything they've said makes total sense. I really need to take the time to figure this all out, before we both get crushed.

Shit . . . Shit . . . Shit . . .

STONE

IT'S ALMOST CRAZY THE WAY that Sage hasn't left my mind once. She's fucking ruined me for anyone else and I honestly don't give two shits who knows.

I may even look like a pussy to the other *W.O.S* guys, but do you think that's going to stop me?

Whether that woman knows it or not; she owns me. My heart is hers to fucking break and I have a feeling that she might do just that.

I could see it in her eyes earlier when I told her how I felt.

She's scared. She's been crushed in the worst way possible in the past. Her and Hemy both.

I'm almost home now and I'm hoping with everything in me that Sage will want to spend the night in my arms, just as she has for the last week.

Everything changed that night in the field. Making love to her only made me fall deeper for her and want with everything in me to show her how much she truly means to me.

So far . . . things have been good. She hasn't kicked me out of her room at night and she's been texting me throughout the day.

Everything about the last week feels like we're in this together. Like we're a couple.

Fuck . . . I don't want this feeling to end.

I walk into the house and look around for Sage. She's not in bed and the whole house is completely dark.

"Fuck . . ." I growl out, while rushing to the back balcony, hoping with everything in me that she's still here.

Relief washes through me when I spot her through the glass door, holding a glass of wine.

She looks up from her chair with a small smile when I slide the door open.

"Hey," she whispers.

"Hey, Babe." I take a seat at the bottom of her chair and place her legs on top of me. "You couldn't sleep?"

She shakes her head and grabs my hand. "I've been thinking all night. I'm not even tired."

Bringing her hand to my lips, I gently kiss it and then pull her into my lap. "You can talk to me, Sage. Please don't be afraid of me."

"It's so hard." She rests her cheek in my hand, when I reach up to cup it. "I'm trying so damn hard, but I'm scared of being hurt, Stone. Having someone that you love abandon you is the worst feeling in the world. I'm not sure I can handle that feeling again."

A tear slides down her cheek, wetting my hand. It hurts so damn much to see her hurting. "Your parents didn't deserve you, Sage. Your father . . ." I pause, trying to figure out the best way to say the next part. "I would've killed him for the way he treated you. His fucking daughter. It's bullshit." My grip on her tightens. "And then he beat Hemy for trying to protect you. Your parents deserve to rot in hell for the shit you've both been through."

"Yeah . . . maybe so, but it still hurts."

"There's no maybe about it, Sage. And your brother. He didn't leave you because he wanted to. It killed him when you two got separated. He was dead without you. Trust me. The only people who abandoned you by choice were the two people who didn't deserve you. I would *never* abandon you. I'd die before hurting you."

She wraps her arms around my neck, burying her face into my neck as the tears come out faster and harder now.

It's killing me inside right now and all I want to do is scream out to her that I love her.

"Stone . . ." She gently kisses my neck. "Will you come to bed with me? I just want you to hold me. Please."

I kiss the top of her head and then wipe my thumbs under her eyes to dry them. "Anything you ask."

Picking her up, I carry her inside and to my bedroom, laying her in my bed, before crawling in behind her.

I wrap my arms around her, pulling her as closely as I can

possibly get her. "Did I ever tell you that my father was a drunk that abandoned me and my mother?"

She shakes her head and kisses my arm. "No. I'm sorry, Stone."

"Don't be. It was the best thing that could've happened to my family. He was an abusive piece of shit that hurt my mom every day. Sometimes the ones that don't deserve you are the ones that leave. Maybe a part of them knows that you deserve better than them. That's how I always looked at it."

"I guess that makes sense," she whispers against my arm. "I guess as a child it's just devastating when it happens. I've been trying to move on from it and let others in, but the fear is still there. The fear of being hurt like that again."

"I get it," I say honestly. As much as I hate to think that she can't trust me yet, I get why it's hard for her to let me in completely.

"Would you be okay with me staying with Jade for a few weeks?"

My heart fucking shatters at the thought of her not being here. It's almost hard to breathe.

"Yeah," I force out. "If you need time then I'll give it to you."

"Thank you." She squeezes my arm and then kisses it. "Goodnight, Stone."

"Goodnight, Beautiful."

As much as I hope that her leaving for a few weeks will be enough to clear her head and really let me in, I'm also afraid that it might be enough space for her to forget me completely.

I can't let that happen . . .

chapter
TWENTY-TWO

STONE

SAGE HAS BEEN GONE FOR two weeks now and it's been eating at me that we haven't talked or spoken since that night.

I'm trying to be a man and give her the time and space that she needs, but every fucking day just gets harder and harder.

"Get out of your fucking head." Styx shoves a shot of whiskey in my face. "You need a few of these."

Wanting nothing more than to clear my thoughts for one fucking second of Sage, I slam the shot back and immediately reach for another as Sara continues to poor them.

"Someone looks a little stressed," Sara says with concern. "Just call her, Stone. I'm sure she's missing you just as much. Hell, she's probably waiting for you to call first. I know how women work."

"Nah." I shake my head and slam the second shot back. "Not her. She asked for space and I'm respecting that. If she missed me . . ." I grab another shot and slam it back, closing my eyes as the liquid slides down my throat, burning it. "She'd be back by now. Or hell . . . she'd at least text."

Styx slaps my back and stands up. "She'll be back. Drink up all you need to get that shit far from your head for now. I'll drive your ass home when you're ready." He messes up my hair and laughs. "I got your back, Bro."

It's been a long time since my ass has gotten wasted, but right now, I just need anything to make me stop thinking about Sage and trying to figure out what she's been thinking since she's been gone.

I've barely slept for shit since the night she packed up some of her shit and left. It's like I keep thinking about how it's going to play out when she decides to come back. Or if she comes back. Different shit plays out in my head every damn night.

I find myself drinking alone when Styx takes off to do his last private dance of the night.

That only makes shit worse, getting me lost in my fucked up thoughts again. Sara's been too busy to stay and talk for me for longer than a few minutes at a time.

Even she is beginning to look concerned with each shot I slam back as if it's water or some shit.

"Okay . . ." She cleans around my half empty beer, before tossing the towel over her shoulder and meeting my eyes. "You've been sitting here in this same damn spot for the last two hours, slamming back shot after shot. You're beginning to look like some fucking loser, Stone. That's not you. You're far from a loser and an asshole."

I close my eyes and take a deep breath, slowly releasing it. I'm fully aware that I probably look like some drunken idiot at the moment, but I just can't seem to give a shit. "I'm fine."

"No the fuck you aren't." She looks pissed when she gets called away to help a group of women. "Drink this water. Got it. Dammit!"

Feeling pissed off at my damn self, I drink the water that Sara threw in front of me and then sit here with my head in my hands.

I stay like this for at least ten minutes, just staring down at my bottle.

"Hey, you." I finally look up when someone sits down beside me and brushes my arm. It's the blonde from a few weeks ago. "You're looking a little lonely over here."

I offer her a faint smile, not wanting to be a dick after what she did for me after her private dance that night. "I guess you can say I have a lot on my mind."

She takes a sip of her mixed drink and looks me over, checking me out. "I saw you from across the bar and thought you could use some company. I'm surprised no other women jumped to the opportunity before me."

I don't. It's the last think that I fucking need, but I'm so drunk right now that I'm afraid I'll say something to upset her or piss her off.

So I just nod my head and tilt back my beer.

"You never called me," she says softly. "I was hoping you would. You just seem so different than most of the men I know. Fun and carefree. I liked that about you."

Trying to get my thoughts in check, I run my hands through my hair and release a breath. I really can't deal with this shit right now. There's too much going on in my head now. "There's a woman that I love and I've been chasing her for over a fucking year. She's the only girl I would've called. Sorry. It's nothing personal."

She looks disappointed, but offers me a small understanding smile anyway. "She's one lucky girl to have *you* chasing her. Where is she?"

I run my thumb over my beer, before tilting it back again. I wish I knew more than anything right now. "I don't know."

That shit burns. Even in my drunken state.

"I'm sorry to hear that." She stands up and places her hands on my face as if to comfort me. "A man like you deserves a woman that will never want to be away from you."

I close my eyes and some fucked up part of me wants to pretend that it's Sage's hands on my face.

Maybe it's because I'm completely fucking drunk at this point and would do anything to be with her.

"I would love to spend my time with you."

Before I know it, her lips are on mine and she's pushing her way in between my legs.

Her hands tangle in the back of my hair, pulling me close to her as she runs her tongue along my bottom lip.

It takes me a few seconds to react, before I pull away from her kiss and remove her hands from my face. "I'm not available," I say stiffly. "Fuck!"

Panic sets in at the realization that another woman's lips have been on mine since Sage's. Even though I didn't want it, it feels like I've just fucking cheated.

The fucked up part is that we're not even a couple. Fuck, I don't even know if she's coming back or not.

"I'm sorry." She backs away and grabs her purse. "I didn't know. It sounded like . . ."

"It's not your fault." I feel guilty as fuck right now. Guilty that another woman kissed me other than Sage and guilty that I've made this woman feel like total shit. "I'm drunk and shit just isn't coming out right."

I call Sara over. She watches me hard, as if she's waiting for what's about to come out of my mouth. I'm not taking this woman home if that's what she fucking thinks. "Please take care of her for me. Bill me later. I need to get my ass out of here and chill out."

Sara gives me a smile as if she's proud of me or some shit. Hell, maybe she is. A lot of men in my situation *would* jump to the opportunity of taking another woman home.

That's not me. Not when I know what I truly want.

Needing to get away from all of the chaos in the bar and calm down, I make my way to the locker room and pull out my phone.

Everything in me wants to text Sage and tell her how much I miss her and want her to come home.

"Fuck!" I punch the wall and then toss my phone aside.

I'm giving her a few more days. I really don't know if I can give her more.

Twenty minutes later, Styx comes in sweaty and out of breath. "Fuck, Dude. You look rough as shit."

"I'm just ready to get the fuck out of here."

"I feel ya. I'll take a quick shower. Just calm your dick and relax a bit."

When Styx drops me off at home, I instantly feel the loss when stepping into the dark, empty house.

I find myself sitting outside on the back balcony until well past five in the damn morning, just thinking about Sage and how we used to sit out here together.

This shit is even harder than I expected . . .

chapter TWENTY-THREE

Sage

IT'S BEEN EXACTLY EIGHTEEN DAYS since I've seen or spoken to Stone now and it's really starting to break me down and wear at my emotions.

I thought leaving would be a good idea and it was. Not because I wanted to be away from Stone, but because a part of me needed to know how much being away from him would kill me.

Being away has shown me just how strong my need for him truly is. It's shown me that it hurts to not hear his voice or see his beautiful face every day.

Now . . . now I just need to figure out if I'm strong enough to give in to my feelings for him, knowing now that losing him will hurt like hell.

If it hurts this much already, I can't even imagine having him as mine and then losing him completely as a partner, roommate and friend.

I spent the first week at Jade's house after I left, but being there just hurt. Especially since all Jade kept talking about was how she wants to go back to the club to see Kash.

Thinking about Kash or Styx only makes me think about Stone even more. I figured she would get that, but her excitement just made her overlook that little fact.

So, I've been here at Hemy's and Onyx's for the last eleven days now, hoping that spending time with family will help me feel less alone. It does, but not enough to make me miss Stone any less.

I threatened Hemy's big ass and made sure he promised me that he wouldn't talk about Stone or tell Stone that I'm staying with them until I'm ready.

He's been pretty good so far, although I can tell he wants talk about it. I think it's finally the time for it, because Stone seems to be the only thing I can think about lately and it's slowly killing me to not get some things off my chest.

Onyx has been asleep for the last two hours, so when the kitchen light turns on, I know that it's Hemy.

Hoping that I can handle talking to him about Stone, I make my way to the kitchen and take a seat at one of the stools.

"Hey, Big brother."

Hemy gives me a tired smile and kisses the side of my head. "What are you doing awake? Don't you work in like five hours?"

I nod my head and watch him tilt back a bottle of water. "Yeah . . . I haven't been sleeping much lately."

"I've noticed and I fucking hate it. Ready to talk about it?" He takes a seat next to me and pulls my stool close to him. "I'm awake until you're good to sleep. Got it."

I take a deep breath and slowly release it. As much as I've been putting it off, I think I need Hemy's advice to move forward.

"I'm scared." I grab his arm and hug it, like how I used to do when we were kids . . . before we got separated. "I care about

Stone so much that the thought of losing him kills me. I remember what it felt like to lose you all those years ago. I couldn't function right for years. What if the same thing happens if I lose Stone?"

He wraps his arm around me and releases a breath. "I wish I could tell you how you will feel if that ever happens, but I can't. I also wish I could tell you it would never happen, but I can't do that either. The one thing I can tell you is that I will always love you and you'll always have me to fall on for support. I will *never* leave you again. Nothing will ever separate us. No matter what happens in the future, you will never be alone, Sage. That's a fucking promise."

He stops to kiss the side of my head again. "I don't know what will happen with you and Stone, but I can tell you that he loves the shit out of you and he's hurting just as much as you are. I may give him shit, but he's a good fucking man and I know he'll treat you like you deserve. I trust him."

I find myself smiling at the fact, that he just admitted what he did. Hemy doesn't trust many people. "You do?"

"Fuck yes, I do. He's one of the few, Sage. That says a lot."

"I love him," I whisper. "A lot."

"I know you do," he whispers back. "It's obvious as shit and it's killing you to be away from him. Now, you just need to let him know it."

I close my eyes and my chest instantly aches at the idea that I could possibly be too late. "It's been over two weeks, Hemy. What if he's given up and moved on already? He's a guy and I know how those fuckers work."

Hemy gives me a small squeeze. "He hasn't. Trust me."

"How do you know?"

"I talked to Sara a few days ago . . ."

My heart begins to beat like crazy in my chest as I wait for him to continue.

"She said that Stone got completely fucking trashed a few days ago."

"And . . ." I push, my heart now beating even faster, afraid of what might come next.

"Some girl kissed him and he pushed her away. Most guys that have moved on, would not push some hot chick away. He'd be taking her ass home and fucking her. We both know it. That should tell you all you need to know."

The thought of another girl's lips on his kills me. It stings like hell, but the fact that he pushed her away, makes my heart happy.

God, I love that man.

He really is something else. He's different.

"That fucker is something else," Hemy says, surprising me. "You should go back home and put you both out of misery. I can't stand to see you both moping around, hurting and shit."

I smile at him when he stands up and yawns. "Thank you for everything. Talking to you somehow always makes me feel better."

He smiles back at me and tiredly rubs his face. "That's what big brothers are for. Right?" He winks and then pulls me in for a tight hug, holding me there for a few minutes. "Love you, Sage."

"I love you too, my big crazy as hell brother." I laugh into his chest.

"Damn straight." He releases me walks out of the kitchen, toward the stairs. "Goodnight. Get some damn sleep now."

"Goodnight," I yell back.

I spend the next hour, replaying our whole conversation in my head and trying to decide what I'm going to do now.

Whatever it is that I decide needs to happen fast. I've put

things off for far too long now and it's hurting the both of us.

My next move could either hurt us more or bring us together.

That scares the hell out of me . . .

chapter TWENTY-FOUR

STONE

YESTERDAY MADE THREE WEEKS SINCE Sage took off and I spent the whole damn night, waiting for her to come home or at least call me and tell me that she wasn't.

I barely slept for shit, because I kept checking my phone every damn hour to see if I missed anything from her.

Not a damn thing and I came close to just throwing my phone and breaking it so that I would stop checking it.

I've decided that I'm giving her until tonight and then I'm going after her. I don't care if she gets pissed. She asked for a few weeks and I gave it to her.

She needs to know exactly how I feel about her.

"Stone! Wait up, Fucker."

I look over to see Kage coming at me. "You have one more private show booked for tonight. Cale told me to have you stay and work it."

"Are you fucking serious? Shit!"

Staying here even longer than I have to is not what the fuck I want to be doing right now.

I was thirty minutes away from getting my ass out of here to go after Sage, and now having to put on a private show will add at least close to an hour to that shit.

"Sorry, Man. Your private door is fucked up right now too so Cale has someone coming in tomorrow afternoon to fix it. Go through the client's door in about ten minutes so you can beat them there."

"Alright, shit. I'm going to take a quick shower then and get this fucking sticky shit off of me. One of the girls spilt their drink down my leg when I picked them up in their damn chair earlier. I haven't had a free minute since."

"I hear ya, Man. Go get that shit cleaned off and hurry. I'll try to hold your client off."

Frustrated as hell, I hurry into the locker room and take a quick shower, before heading into my private room.

It's completely dark and if I'm not mistaken, I see a body move from on the stage in front of what looks to be a pole.

When the fuck did my private room get a pole?

It's too dark to see, but I even smell some sweet perfume. I'm definitely not alone in here and fuck me, they smell like Sage. I'd recognize that sweet smell from anywhere.

Out of nowhere, *Close* by Nick Jonas begins playing over the speakers and the stage lights up enough for me to see Sage, standing there looking completely sexy as fuck.

Standing with her back against the pole, she brings one arm back to wrap around it, and slowly lowers her body down the pole, while rubbing her other hand down the center of her body, over the black lace. Once she gets close to the ground, she spreads her knees apart and lowers her hand some more, biting her bottom lip as she touches herself through the fabric.

My cock instantly hardens as she watches me with a

seductive look in her eyes as if she wants nothing more than to make love to me right here.

Fuck, I want that more than anything right now and it's going to take everything in me not to take her right here, right now.

She sways her hips to the rhythm of the music, releasing the pole, and wrapping her hands in her hair, tugging as she makes her way back up the pole in a stance.

I can't take my fucking eyes off of her. It's been a long time since I've seen her dance. But watching her now, brings me back to the beginning when I first saw her on the stage at *Vixens* and wanted nothing more than to just taste her body.

I want to taste it now.

Slowly turning around, she wraps one leg around the pole and arches her back, swinging her long hair around, before gripping the pole and spinning around it, seductively. Her moves are so smooth and in control that you would never think that she stopped dancing over a year ago.

She spins around a few times, moving seductively to the music, before releasing the pole, walking to the edge of the small stage, and reaching for the ribbon that's holding her black corset together.

Keeping her eyes on me, she lowers herself to the surface of the stage, down to her ass, and spreads her legs wide apart, revealing the sheer, black lace that's in between.

Biting her bottom lip, she slightly tugs the ribbon, opening her top a little more, and rolling her hips up and down with her back pressed the against the stage.

Out of instinct, I reach out and run my hands up her legs, pulling her to me. Breathing heavily, I lean in to her ear. "Fuck, I missed you." I brush her hair behind her ear and gently kiss up her neck. "You're so fucking beautiful, Sage. I'm glad you're here."

She grips my hair with both hands and places her forehead against mine. "I'm not going to lie. I missed you too, Stone. Not a minute went by that I didn't want to come back home and be with you."

Her words cause relief to wash through me. I've waited for what feels like forever to hear those words and I was beginning to think that I lost her completely. "I'm still waiting," I whisper. "I haven't gone anywhere."

With desperation, she presses her lips against mine and wraps her arms so tightly around my neck that it almost hurts.

It's almost as if she was afraid of losing me too.

I love the feeling. This feeling right here is so worth the last three weeks of suffering that I went through without her.

Fuck, I love her so much.

Standing up, I pick her up with me, walking over to press her back up against the wall.

Holding her up with my hips, I tangle my hands in her hair and kiss her deep and hard, causing her to moan into my mouth.

"Fuck, Sage. I'm trying so hard not to be rough with you right now, but I'm fucking dying to be inside you right now."

"I never asked you to be gentle," she whispers against my lips. "Fuck me like you love me."

With force, I press my hips into her and growl against her mouth. "I do . . . fucking love you."

Her grip on me tightens and her eyes widen as she looks up at me. "Do you mean that? I mean . . . are you sure? I just left for three–."

"Hell yes, I mean it, Sage. You could leave me for a year and it wouldn't change the fact that you're the only woman I've ever loved."

"Are you sure you want to love me?" She asks with fear in her eyes.

I hate that look.

"More than anything in this fucking world," I say firmly.

With urgency, I rip her panties off, before sliding my jeans down my hips and pushing into her hard and deep.

She moans out and digs her nails into my back, hard. So hard that there's no doubt that I'm bleeding right now.

"Oh shit, Stone . . ." she breathes into my ear. "I've missed you inside of me. I've missed us. You have no idea."

"Oh, I do. Trust me." I slowly pull out of her, before slamming back into her and stilling. "I missed us too, Baby. Everything about us. Don't ever fucking leave me again. Please."

"I won't," she breathes. "Because I love you too."

"Oh fuck . . ." My grip on her tightens and my body becomes desperate to take her as deeply as I can. I can't get enough of the beautiful woman right now. "Best news I've heard in my entire life. That's the truth."

I kiss her deep and hard, while continuing to thrust inside of her for what feels like hours. We're completely covered in sweat now, but there's no way I'm stopping.

Pulling away from her lips, I wrap my hand around her throat and push myself deeper inside of her, causing her to shake in my arms. "Fuck, I only want this with you." I pull her bottom lip into my mouth and bite into as I start thrusting hard and fast again, pushing her up the wall with each movement.

I reach down and grab her hands, binding them in one hand, and raising them above her head. Both of us are breathing heavy, me holding her hands above her head while holding her up with my opposite arm supporting her waist.

"Me too, Stone. Oh fuck!" She pulls back on my hair as I push into her one last time, feeling my orgasm build before I release myself deep inside her.

Not even seconds later, she's shaking in my arms, her own orgasm causing her to scream my out my name and yank on my hair.

I hold her in my arms for as long as I can, before setting her down on the leather couch and dropping to my knees in front of her.

"You ready to go home now?" I kiss the side of her head, before kissing her lips. "Please fucking say yes."

I sound desperate, but I don't give a shit right now. I am desperate.

She wraps her arms around me and buries her face into my sweaty neck. "There's nowhere else I want to be. I'm miserable without your cocky ass and your dick pics."

We both smile, before bursting into laughter.

This woman truly is perfect for me and I'm taking her home where she belongs.

WE SPEND THE REST OF the night outside on the back balcony, her in my arms as we just talk about life and joke around.

When you have the W.O.S. crew in your life, there's plenty of shit to talk about and laugh over.

I've never smiled so much in my life than I do when I'm with Sage. She's everything I could ask for in my life and more.

I have a feeling that we'll be spending a lot of long nights out here, looking at the stars and getting to know everything about each other.

Now that I have her heart, you're damn straight that I'll be doing everything in my power to keep it and show her how much I truly love her.

I smile when I look down to see her falling asleep in my arms. She's practically holding onto to me for dear life as if she never wants to let go.

Well, I never want her to and she'll never have to . . .

chapter
TWENTY-FIVE

Sage

FIVE WEEKS LATER

STYX HAS BEEN RUNNING AROUND the back yard, fighting anyone who even dares to go close to the precious grill.

It's Stone's fucking grill and even he's not allowed to touch it, without getting Styx's wrath.

"Damn, that man's fucking crazy when he's cooking. The asshole threw a hot ass hot dog at my lip." He touches his lip as if it hurts. "Remind me not to invite his ass next time.

I can't help but to laugh as Stone takes a seat beside me and looks over at Styx manning the grill and guarding it with his life.

"Next time we'll have to tie him up so he won't be able to go near it. How about?" I tease, while gently kissing his bottom lip.

"Hell. No." He pulls me into his lap and kisses me, harder. "He'd like it way too much being tied up. Trust me. Not happening."

Styx must be listening to our conversation, because when I

look up at him, he winks and takes a bite of a kabob. He somehow makes it look extremely sexy. Must be a Walk Of Shame
thing.

"I think you're right." I laugh.

"Fuck yeah, he is, Babe." Styx opens the grill and begins flipping the food. "But I'll still let you if you want. His ass might like
to watch."

"Fuck off, Asshole, before I stab your dick with that tem-
perature fork. We'll see what the hell you can do with your dick
after that."

"What the fuck?" Styx growls. "That shit isn't even cool."
He covers his dick and goes back to catering to the food.

The boys continue to banter back and forth, Kash somehow
finding a way to jump in and rile them up even more.

I swear I don't know what to do with them some days.

Hemy and Onyx arrive, grabbing my attention and not even
ten minutes later, Cale, Riley and baby Haven show up.

Slade, Aspen and Kash have been here since even before the
food started cooking and Sara should be arriving here soon too.

Slade and Aspen somehow managed to slip away to who
knows where over twenty minutes ago, but no one has bothered
to look. As long as they clean up their mess when they're done,
then they're welcome to go as crazy as they want.

It's the Fourth of July so Cale and Aspen made plans to shut
down their businesses for the day so that we could all be here
together.

It makes my heart so happy to have us all here in one place.
It never gets to happen anymore and I miss it more than I even
knew.

These people are my family and the more time I spend with
them, the more I love them and grow to trust them.

Especially Stone. I never thought I'd ever be able to trust

a man as much as I do my brother, but Stone just continues to prove me wrong with each and every day.

The truth is, he's been showing me for over a year now. I was just too blind to see it, afraid of getting myself hurt.

We've officially been a couple for over a month now and there's no doubt in my mind that I made the right decision by letting him in.

There's no way I'll be running off to be away from him again.

I just have to make sure that I continue to show him that.

I'm quickly learning that I love him more than I could've ever imagined . . .

"Are you fucking crazy? My shit never gets old. Let's go right now and have the girls judge."

When I look away from talking with the girls, Stone is standing on top of the picnic table, looking as if he's ready to strip down to his boxer briefs.

"Get your ass down," Slade complains, when he finally reappears with Aspen under his arm. "No one wants to see you shake your dick."

"Thank fucking goodness." Kash throws his empty soda can Stone's way. "We're not at the club. I want to take the night and enjoy the sight of anything *but* Stone and Styx's dicks swinging."

Stone smirks and jumps down from the table. "Alright . . . It's not like we need to dance to prove who's better anyway. I'll save you dicks some embarrassment."

Hemy looks away from baby Haven laying in his huge arms. She's looks like a baby doll compared to Hemy. "Come on, Fucktards. There's a baby here."

Onyx slaps Hemy's leg and then leans in to bite his neck. "Yeah, so watch your mouth, Sexy."

"Hey, Bitches!"

Everyone looks over at the sound of Sara's voice. She pokes her head through the fence and laughs, before walking in and guiding some chick with her.

"Hey, Babe," I smile when Sara entwines her fingers with the girl and pulls her close to her side. "Who's your friend?"

Sara seems to have everyone's attention now.

"Stop staring and shit, jeez." Sara grabs the girl by the back of the head and presses her lips against hers. Then she turns around to face us. "My date. Now you've seen us kiss." She points to the guys. "So don't even bother asking us to do it again and stare like idiots."

The guys seem pretty impressed with Sara's taste and I definitely don't blame them. This chick is hot.

I guess there's a lot about Sara that I don't know yet.

"Congrats on the book, Babe." Sara kisses my cheek and then introduces me to Kendal.

Kendal seems really nice and interested in what my books are about. I already like this chick.

Time seems to fly by after we eat and by the time eight o'clock rolls around, everyone is playing Cornhole and waiting for it to get dark enough to shoot off fireworks.

I'm just about to take my turn, when Stone picks me up from behind and starts swirling me around.

"Stop!" I laugh and slap at his hands, until he puts me down and kisses me. "Stop trying to make me dizzy so you and Styx win. Not cool!"

He smiles against my lips, before pressing his lips to mine and smothering me in his strong arms. "You know I don't play fair," he says against my neck."

Sara whistles from across the yard at us. "Come on you two!"

Stone pulls away and cups my face in his hands. His face

lights up as the fireworks begin shooting off above us. "I love you," he says loudly enough for me to hear.

Hearing him say those three words still makes my heart go just as crazy as it did when he said them five weeks ago.

I don't think I'll ever get tired of those words coming from his beautiful lips.

This man has become my world . . .

STONE

"I LOVE YOU, TOO. SO damn much and I don't plan on stopping anytime soon, Stone."

Forgetting all about the game, I pull her against me and hold her tightly, as we watch the firework display above us.

It's so fucking beautiful and having her here in my arms only makes the moment that much more perfect. I honestly couldn't ask for anything better right now.

Not to mention that our whole family is here to enjoy it with us.

It somehow just makes it feel that much more complete.

By the time the fireworks are over, everyone has pretty much forgotten about the game and any other activity everyone was involved in.

We all somehow find our way around the fire pit, roasting marshmallows and telling stories and jokes.

Styx attempts to tell a drunken story that he claims to be true, but that somehow turns into a joke too, everyone laughing and making fun of him for hours.

We don't end up making it inside until well after midnight

and I have to admit that I've been dying to get Sage alone and hold her in some peace and quiet.

Sage doesn't waste any time stripping down to her sheer top that I love so much and a pair of panties, before grabbing a blanket and making her way outside on the balcony.

I strip down myself getting damn excited to finally be close to her, now that everyone's gone.

When I follow her outside, she pulls me down onto the lounge chair, between her legs and kisses my arm.

Getting comfortable, I cup her face in my hands and press my forehead to hers. "Do you have any idea how much I love you?"

She nods her head and laughs. "I have a pretty good idea, but I won't mind if you continue to keep reminding me, daily." She smiles against my lips, before kissing me, hard as if she's missed me all day. "Lay down with me. There's still random fireworks going off. I want to enjoy them with only you."

Shifting us around, so that she's positioned between my legs now, I securely wrap my arms around her and just hold her.

As much as I love making love to her, holding her in moments like this, means so much more at times.

It reminds me that what we have is deeper and I plan to make that last with everything in me.

This woman has my heart in her hands and I don't plan on asking for it back . . .

The end of #1

If you enjoyed Stone (Walk Of Shame 2nd Generation #1) and want more of the dirty boys of Walk Of Shame, be sure to check out the first generation: Slade, Hemy and Cale available on Amazon.

acknowledgements

First and foremost, I'd like to say a big thank you to all of my loyal readers that have given me support over the last couple of years and have encouraged me to continue with my writing. Your words have all inspired me to do what I enjoy and love. Each and every one of you mean a lot to me and I wouldn't be where I am if it weren't for your support and kind words.

I'd also like to thank my beta readers, Amy Preston Rogers, Hetty Rasmussen, Kellie Richardson, Justine Mcfadyen and Keeana Porter. I love you ladies and appreciate you taking the time to read my words.

My amazingly, wonderful PA, Amy Preston Rogers. She helped me from the very beginning of Stone and fell in love with him before anyone else. Her support has meant so much to me.

I'd like to thank another friend of mine, Clarise Tan from *CT Cover Creations* for creating my cover. You've been wonderful to work with and have helped me in so many ways.

Thank you to my boyfriend, friends and family for understanding my busy schedule and being there to support me through the hardest part. I know it's hard on everyone, and everyone's support means the world to me.

Last but not least, I'd like to thank all of the wonderful book bloggers that have taken the time to support my book and help spread the word. You all do so much for us authors and it is greatly appreciated. I have met so many friends on the way and you guys are never forgotten. You guys rock. Thank you!

about the author

Victoria Ashley grew up in Rockford, IL and has had a passion for reading for as long as she can remember. After finding a reading app where it allowed readers to upload their own stories, she gave it a shot and writing became her passion.

She lives for a good romance book with tattooed bad boys that are just highly misunderstood and is not afraid to be caught crying during a good read. When she's not reading or writing about bad boys, you can find her watching her favorite shows such as Supernatural, Sons Of Anarchy and The Walking Dead.

She is the author of Wake Up Call, This Regret, Slade, Hemy, Cale, Get Off On The Pain, Something For The Pain, Thrust, Royal Savage and is currently working on more works for 2016.

CONTACT HER AT:
www.victoriaashleyauthor.com
Facebook
Twitter: @VictoriaAauthor
Intstagram: VictoriaAshley.Author

books by
victoria ashley